PENROSS MANOR

OTHER BOOKS BY JOAN WINMILL BROWN

No Longer Alone
Wings of Joy
Every Knee Shall Bow
Corrie: The Lives She's Touched
Day by Day with Billy Graham
Together Each Day
Christmas Joys
The Martyred Christian —Dietrich Bonhoeffer
Joy in His Presence
Never Alone
Another Love
Love's Tender Journey
Let Me Love Again
If Love Be Ours

JOAN WINMILL BROWN
PENROSS MANOR

WORD BOOKS
PUBLISHER
WACO, TEXAS

A DIVISION OF
WORD, INCORPORATED

PENROSS MANOR

Library of Congress Cataloging in Publication Data:

Brown, Joan Winmill.
    Penross Manor.

    I. Title.
PS3552.R68568P46   1986   813'.54   86-9104
ISBN 0-8499-0517-6

    Printed in the United States of America

    67898 BKC 987654321

Batter my heart, three-personed God; for you
As yet but knock, breathe, shine, and seek to mend.
That I may rise and stand, o'erthrow me and bend
Your force to break, blow, burn, and make me new.
I, like an usurped town, to another due,
Labor to admit you, but, oh, to no end;
Reason, your viceroy in me, me should defend,
But is captived and proves weak or untrue.

Yet dearly I love you and would be loved fain,
But am betrothed unto your enemy:
Divorce me, untie or break that knot again,
Take me to you, imprison me, for I,
Except you enthrall me, never shall be free,
Nor ever chaste, except you ravish me.

—JOHN DONNE

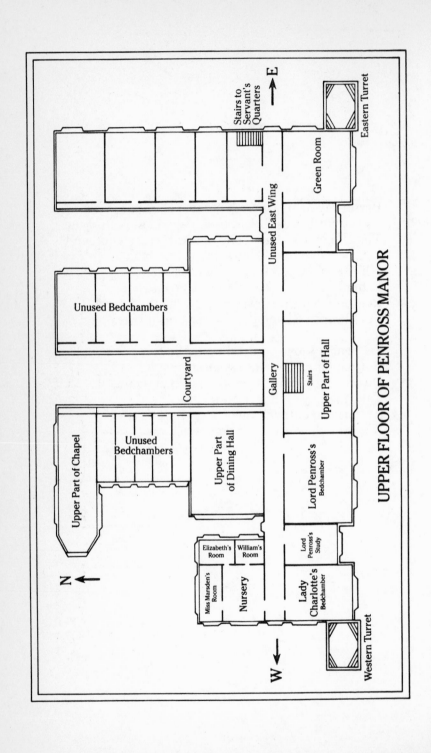

UPPER FLOOR OF PENROSS MANOR

N

W

E

Western Turret

Eastern Turret

Upper Part of Chapel

Unused Bedchambers

Courtyard

Unused Bedchambers

Stairs to Servant's Quarters

Unused East Wing

Green Room

Upper Part of Dining Hall

Gallery

Upper Part of Hall

Stairs

Lord Penross's Bedchamber

Lord Penross's Study

Miss Marsden's Room

Nursery

Elizabeth's Room

William's Room

Lady Charlotte's Bedchamber

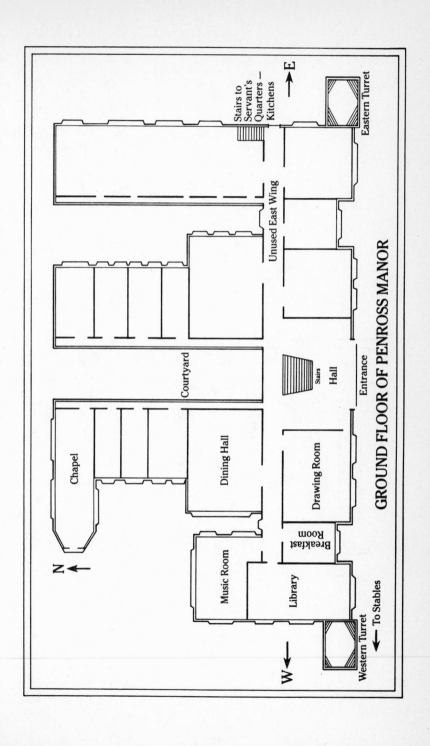

GROUND FLOOR OF PENROSS MANOR

1

Resisting the galelike winds that had pounded its sides for the last few miles, the coach shuddered and almost came to a stop. Seated inside, I heard the horses' defiant neighing and the crack of the coachman's whip, and I longed to take it from his vicious hands. He was in an evil mood.

Upon his arrival at my house in London, the coachman had presented himself with a cursory touch of his hat and had muttered defiantly that Lord James Penross's coach awaited me.

With an almost uncontrollable surge of emotion, I had said farewell to Jenkins, our family's old servant. He had known me as a child and had seen the Winton fortune gradually dwindle to its present, paltry state. Some years before, it had been necessary to sell our country estate, and unless a miracle happened my brother Stephen and I were in jeopardy of losing our London home. In social circles I was now described as a "distressed gentlewoman."

Out of love, and feeling it more than my duty, I had cared for my mother—missing perhaps many of the gratifications of a busy social life. With her death, five years after my father's, had come the added responsibility of the house and the prospect of facing—at twenty-six years of age—a lonely future.

I had walked through the memory-filled rooms, now covered with dust-sheets, and said a silent farewell to the home

I had known all my life. And my aunt's consoling voice had come back to me: "My dear Charlotte, it is all for the best. With your mother's death this will help ease the loneliness." Lady Sanford, my mother's spinster sister, had continued, "Lord Penross's children will love you, and you will be helping to bring some happiness into their lives. It has not been easy for them since they, too, lost their mother. . . ."

Pausing at the top step outside my house, I had looked up and down the street. A carriage swept by and a gentleman I knew doffed his hat. I waved, wondering if he knew that I was now beginning a journey into what for me was unknown territory. Lord Penross's manor house was nearly three hundred miles away in Cornwall—a county rife with legend and folklore. I might as well be crossing the Atlantic; it seemed so far distant . . .

Now only Jenkins was left to guard my home. His old, rheumy eyes had watered as mine did as he said, "Safe trip, m'lady. Don't worry about the 'ouse—I'll take good care of it."

The coach had pulled out into Park Lane, and I had looked out on a London bedecked for spring. Daffodils were blooming in Hyde Park, and the sturdy blossoms seemed to wave a silent farewell in the balmy breeze. The luxurious interior of Lord Penross's coach had become my interim refuge. I had leant my head against the blue velvet upholstery and allowed the pent-up tears to flow . . .

A sudden violent lurch brought me back to the present. We had now been traveling for four nightmarish days, having stopped for the night in several questionable inns, each one noisier than the last. Sleep had evaded me, and I longed for the end of the journey.

On hearing of my destination, the innkeeper at the King's Head in Plymouth had shaken his head and said, ominously, "In those parts it's 'ard to sort out what is idle gossip and what is the truth."

His wife had knowingly whispered, "I wouldn't want no daughter of mine living there."

I had asked them to explain, but the innkeeper had hushed his wife as she was about to speak. "There's beds to be made—no time for talking, woman. . . ."

I had brushed aside their remarks, remembering how quickly gossip spreads its vicious tentacles and becomes, in many cases, blatant untruth. But now, as the howling winds rocked the coach, I found it difficult not to dwell on their words.

The journey had worsened by the hour. Finally, as we crossed the county line into Cornwall, a storm that had been brewing out to sea broke loose with a fury I scarce remembered seeing before. The coach now seemed too fragile to withstand such a buffeting, and I found myself praying that we would arrive safely at Penross Manor.

In the darkness, I felt for the small valise beside me and reached inside, searching for the brass carriage clock that had belonged to my mother. It was impossible to see its porcelain face, so I pressed the small striker button. It chimed the nearest hour—nine o'clock. With difficulty, but with a certain amount of relief, I returned the clock to the valise—even while hanging on for dear life to the strap near the window. The coachman had predicted we would arrive at Penross Manor before ten o'clock. At least the end of the journey was in sight.

Driving rain was now beating against the windows of the coach, and as we drove through a small village all I could see was a distorted impression of a few cottages nestled together. The lights in their windows swept past me—a welcome respite from the pitch darkness that increased my doubts of whether this new venture was a wise one.

My aunt, Lady Sanford, had recommended to Lord Penross that I help take charge of his two small children. "It will not be as if you were a servant, Charlotte. Your status in society forbids that. No, you will become one of the family, as it were. With your gifts for music and language . . . the children will be fortunate indeed."

It had seemed a rational decision to make, several months after my mother's funeral . . .

And then I was remembering once more that sad day—the rain beating down on the coach that transported me to the bleak, drenched graveyard. Standing beneath an umbrella, with my brother Stephen's arm around me, I had listened to the dour, unbending minister intone the funeral service. There had been no words of comfort. No hope. Mother had taught us that death was only a beginning, but looking at that man's stern, forbidding face, my faith had shattered and almost died.

Stephen had sensed my added desolation, and his arm had tightened around my shoulders. Dressed in the scarlet uniform of the Coldstream Guards, he had looked so noble and strong. If only he were with me now—but his regiment had been on alert since Napoleon's recent escape from the Isle of Elba. It was rumored that the Frenchman was already recruiting an army, and that once more England faced an interminable war . . .

My coach had passed only fifty or so miles north of Southampton, as it took me ever onward to Penross Manor. I wondered how long it would be before Stephen and his regiment would have to sail from that great port for the Continent.

"Dear God, keep him safe!"

A few drops of rain managed to squeeze through the sides of the carriage window, and instinctively I drew my cloak more tightly around me. The velvet blanket, lined in fur and embroidered with the Penross crest, felt damp; in the darkness, I brushed away the raindrops and edged farther away from the window.

The carriage continued to sway, and the ruts in the muddied road made it shudder and reel. Again I heard the angry cry of the coachman and the crack of his whip. The horses stumbled in the mud, and he cursed them for their clumsiness.

There was a violent flash of lightning as the coach turned down toward the coast. For a split second, I could see a brilliant panoramic view. The sea was crashing against unrelenting granite cliffs, upon which stood a vast mansion, proudly dominating the coastline.

" 'Tis the manor, m'lady!" I barely heard the muffled voice of the coachman as the wild winds snatched the sound away.

I hoped for another flash of lightning, so that I could see once more the beautiful yet strangely foreboding architecture. Imprinted on my mind were two high turrets, seemingly Elizabethan in their design.

We were now driving through another small village, and

again there was a glimmer of light from some of the houses. Then I felt us ascending a hill, and my heart began to beat wildly. I was nearing the end of my journey. I almost wished I could order the coach turned around and return posthaste to London.

Another flash of lightning revealed a graveyard beside a small Norman, granite church. Large, towering trees fringed the gray carpet of gravestones. What must be the rectory had a welcoming light in one of the rooms. Momentarily, I saw a simply furnished living room and someone sitting by the fire, reading a large book.

The carriage turned into a driveway, which wound up the hill. We were passing through large wrought-iron gates, adorned with the Penross crest. Above were two lions rampant—their paws raised as if waiting to attack any would-be trespasser.

After several minutes, the sound of the horses' hoofs digging down into the loose gravel of the courtyard caused me to look out. Large, gracious windows were illuminated before me. I gasped out loud; I had traveled so long in almost total darkness that the glowing house dazzled me. The silhouette of its turrets and gabled entrance gave promise to one of the most resplendent buildings I had ever encountered.

The coachman got down from his perch and begrudgingly came to open the door of the coach. I caught once more his look of disdain, but nevertheless thanked him.

Even though it was still raining, I paused for a moment in alighting and gazed up once more at the stately turrets. Then a chill ran through me. Silhouetted in a leaded-paned window at the very top of one of the turrets was the figure of a man, peering down at me . . .

I looked away for a moment, as the coachman handed me an umbrella, then back again. The window was now in darkness.

Had I imagined I had seen a man?

The words of the innkeeper and his wife came back to me once more: "In those parts it's 'ard to sort out what is idle gossip and what is the truth . . ." "I wouldn't want no daughter of mine living there . . ." And the great house, which moments before had seemed warm and welcoming, now seemed pervaded by an eerie strangeness.

11

The coachman's voice, telling me to hurry into the house, made me realize I was still standing in the rain. Overcoming the impulse to look once more at the turret, I turned and walked resolutely up the steps leading to the great, elaborately carved front door. But as I did, I longed with all my being to return to my familiar home in London.

2

The immense doors of Penross Manor swung open, and I was greeted by a tall, distinguished man, his immaculately groomed white hair framing a stern, unbending face.

His words were icily polite: "Good evening, Lady Charlotte. Welcome to Penross. I am Rogers, Lord Penross's butler." He turned and bade a young footman carry my luggage to the Green Room in the east wing.

For a brief moment I saw the coachman scowl and look questioningly at Rogers, who turned to me, apologetically.

"I regret that because of the storms we have been experiencing, the room Lord Penross requested for you has been damaged, Lady Charlotte. It should be repaired in a few days. Until then, I am sure you will find the Green Room more than comfortable."

With a quick word of gratitude, I followed him up the wide, sweeping staircase, trying to take in the beauty of the great white marble hall. It was surrounded by what must be family portraits; their disdainful eyes seemed to follow me as I ascended. The lofty cupola ceiling, painted and gilded in a highly rococo style, added to the feeling of opulence.

At the top of the staircase, the butler turned to the right and proceeded to walk down a long, dark gallery lit by only a few candelabra and lined by forbidding suits of armor. I looked back down to the brightness of the entry hall and saw that the coachman was still standing there, his eyes seeming to bore right through me. With a nod I acknowledged him and started quickly after the butler.

"This wing is not frequently used, Lady Charlotte; in fact, it has been unoccupied for some time. Since Lady Penross's death, his lordship has not entertained on a grand scale. However, your room has been aired, and I trust you will find everything to your liking."

He stopped outside a door almost at the end of the corridor, and from a large brass ring he selected the appropriate key. The young footman was already standing there with some of my luggage, and he stepped aside while the door was unlocked.

It occurred to me to wonder why the room was kept locked.

Pushing open the door, Rogers ushered me inside the room. It was pitch dark.

"Forgive me, Lady Charlotte. The servants should have seen to it that you were not welcomed to your bedchamber in darkness."

I waited for what seemed a few seconds, and then the room was gradually bathed in light. The candles cast a gentle glow on the oak paneling, and I saw that the furnishings were somber and dark. The four-poster bed was hung with deep-green brocade, and the only chair that looked remotely comfortable was upholstered in the same material. A large portrait over the fireplace was of a gentleman from the Elizabethan period; he reminded me of the harsh minister who had presided at my mother's funeral. I was glad to know that my stay in this room would be a short one.

"I had given orders for a fire to have been lit, Lady Charlotte. I apologize. It shall be done immediately."

I thanked him and was relieved when he and the boy left the room. Removing my bonnet, I shook my head and ran my fingers through my hair; it felt grimy from the long journey. I glanced over at my small valise, wishing to find my hairbrush, but decided to wait until the fire had been lit. The room was bone-chilling cold, and I drew my long cape around me before walking over to the window.

The darkness outside was complete; all I could see was my own reflection and that of the uninviting room behind me. A wave of homesickness swept over me. My own bedroom was papered in bright daffodil yellow, with delicate Hepplewhite furniture. I longed to hear the sound of the horses' hoofs as they conveyed the carriages down the street to Hyde Park. The remembered austerity of Rogers—as compared to my dear old servant, Jenkins—caused a tear to form, which I hastily brushed aside.

The storm had now stopped, and the awesome quietness of this great house made me strain to hear at least the noise of an owl or some other creature in the vast grounds. But there was nothing—only the muffled pounding of the sea nearby—and again I felt a chill go through me. I knew I would not be able to stand the isolation of Penross Manor for long. In the morning I would tell Lord Penross I could only stay for a short time.

There was a light knock on my door, and when I called out, "Enter!" the young footman came in, carrying a heavy scuttle of coal. He set it down noisily by the fireplace and shook his hands.

" 'Tis heavy, m'lady," and proceeded to make a large fire, while whistling under his breath a doleful melody. After a few false starts the fire began to blaze, and he stepped back to admire his handiwork.

"There, m'lady; that should make the room a little warmer."

I thanked him, and asked his name. "Tom, m'lady. Me mother's the 'ousekeeper. She'll be up shortly with somethin' to eat." He crossed the room and was about to leave when he asked hopefully, "You'll not be needing the large trunks this evenin'?"

I shook my head and he left, still whistling. In spite of the late hour, he seemed happy to have been of service; his round, ruddy face bore a constant, ingenuous smile. After having experienced the coachman's contempt and the haughtiness of the butler, I was thankful for Tom.

My valises had been opened and left on two luggage racks. I decided I would only unpack what was absolutely necessary. If I were to be moved to another room shortly, or if I decided I could not bear to remain at Penross, my luggage would be ready for departure.

There was another knock on the door, and in came a smiling yet distant woman of about forty years of age. She bore a large tray laden with several covered dishes—and the welcome sight of a teapot. Her white mob cap was perched atop a flutter of dark hair, streaked with gray, that looked as if it could never be trained to lie down with any degree of order. Her piercing brown eyes searched mine, as if questioning who this new addition to the household was and how I was reacting to my new quarters.

"I'm Mrs. Dawson, Lord Penross's 'ousekeeper, and I welcome ye, Lady Charlotte, to our parts. I've taken the liberty to bring ye a light supper. I thought as 'ow ye would be starved from the journey. Was it a rough one? Must 'ave been, what with the terrible storm . . ."

Mrs. Dawson proceeded to chatter without giving me any chance to respond. She laid a white cloth over a small table by the fireplace and quickly set my meal upon it.

"There!" Mrs. Dawson stepped back to make sure that everything was in place. "Would ye be liking me to serve yer soup, yer ladyship?"

I hastily told her that I would serve myself, and that I appreciated the meal. I had last eaten over six hours ago, and I was feeling a trifle faint. But gnawing deep inside me, far more than hunger, was my longing for home.

I waited for Mrs. Dawson to leave, but she stood by the door and carried on talking.

"The children are anxious to meet ye in the morning, yer ladyship. Lord Penross 'as retired for the night, but looks forward to seeing ye at breakfast—which is served promptly at eight o'clock. 'Ot water will be delivered to ye at seven o'clock. Is there anything else ye wish? Would ye like me to unpack for ye? Because of an emergency, yer maid 'ad the day off. She went in to Falmouth to see 'er mother, who is poorly . . ."

Not wanting to faint dead away before her eyes for want of food, I politely interrupted her, saying I did not need her services and would look forward to meeting Lord Penross and the children in the morning.

She closed the door; I sank thankfully onto the chair by the fire and proceeded to serve the hot, steaming soup. The welcome thick broth began to restore my strength, and the homemade bread and Cornish butter soon helped fill the void.

The flames continued to dance around the coal, and gradually the awful chill began to leave the lofty, dank room. I caught sight of myself in the large armoire mirror. My blonde hair did indeed look dirty, and my eyes were smudged with dark shadows. It was then that I realized how exhausted I really was. As soon as I finished my meal, I would prepare for bed—even though the mattress looked lumpy. I was thankful that a warming pan had been placed between the sheets. At least something had been done to welcome me to this remote and uninviting room.

Once more the absolute quiet disturbed me. Perhaps in time I would become used to the silence.

Reaching for the small silver teapot, I poured myself some of the warming brew. Then I sat back in my chair, thinking of the exhausting journey I had just experienced and of what would lie ahead tomorrow when I met Lord Penross and the children. I was beginning an entirely new life, and I prayed that it would be a satisfying one.

The thought of Lord Penross made me wonder why he had not waited up to greet me. Perhaps he was an early riser, as I had been told Cornish people were. But his absence nevertheless seemed rather inhospitable.

Could it have been Lord Penross who had looked down at me from the turret when I arrived? A shudder went through me, remembering the face. I had met Lord Penross when I was only fourteen years of age. He had been at my aunt's house, and I had been briefly introduced to him, then told to join the children in the nursery. My impression was of a tall, dark, brooding man—austerely handsome. But not like the face in the window—no, he surely could not have grown quite so sinister-looking over the years . . .

I poured myself more tea and warmed my hands around the cup. The apple pie was yet to be devoured, but I was in no hurry now. Drowsily I sipped the tea, and was about to set the cup down, when I heard a distinct "click" that seemed to come from the paneling across the room.

It was then that I felt I was not alone. I sat petrified, staring into the fire.

In my mind, I frantically retraced the long walk down the dark corridor from the top of the stairs. Could this room be next to the turret where I had seen the sinister figure peering down at me?

Again, I heard the "click."

The teacup slipped from my hand and crashed upon the saucer. I stifled a cry, and prayed for help . . .

3

Sitting completely rigid, still looking into the fire, I summoned all the strength I had and turned to look in the direction from whence I had heard the strange noise.

I thought I could see now the distinct outline of a door slightly ajar in the paneling. A power outside of myself helped me stand. My hands and legs were shaking, but I determined to walk toward the paneling. (Even as a child, I had had a fatalistic curiosity—as if facing the unknown would drive away whatever evil presence lay waiting for me.)

I leant against the paneling and listened. The wild beating of my heart made it difficult for me to discern whether it was only my imagination—or did I really hear someone breathing heavily behind the door?

Two feet away was a low oak chest. With all the strength I had, I managed to push it against the paneling—barricading the door which had become apparent. I stood there, silently waiting to see whether the door would come ajar again, but to my relief it remained closed.

I slowly walked backward, not daring to take my eyes off the paneling, until I reached the bed and held on to one of the posts. An icy terror now gripped me, sending chills throughout my whole body. I knew I must keep my head and not faint, even though my knees were buckling beneath me.

"Dear God, help me, help me," I repeated over and over again.

There was absolute silence.

I went over to my two valises; and, after closing them, heaved them onto the top of the chest. Once more, I listened, but I could hear nothing.

Relieved, I saw by the fireplace a bell-pull which would summon one of the servants. I ran toward it and took it in my hands. But the bell-pull fell from the wall, and I could see that it had been dismantled.

At that point the enormity of my isolation overwhelmed me. Hurrying over to the door leading out of the bedchamber, I opened it and peered down the long corridor. It was completely dark, the candles having been extinguished. I did not know where in the great house to go for help, and the thought of running down the long, dark corridor frightened me even more than staying in the room.

I closed the door and leant against it, asking that God would give me wisdom—and courage—to face this night alone. Above all, I had to keep a light burning. I counted the candles. There were now six alight, and another six had been placed on a table by the bed. If I kept only one burning, there should be ample supply to last until dawn broke.

The fire was beginning to sink lower into the grate, and there was only one bucket of coal, but I noticed some logs in a separate container. If I were careful, I could have the illumination from the fire also. The thought of undressing for the night was out of the question, and after extinguishing all the candles save the one by my bed, I took off my shoes and huddled underneath the sheets—listening—afraid that I might hear the clicking sound coming from the paneling once more.

I kept the warming pan beside me, for its heat was most welcome and helped alleviate the terrible chills. But why had the servants remembered to place it in the bed, yet not lit the fire—or the candles?

Was it because of the late hour I was allowing my imagination to play tricks on me? There was probably a perfectly plausible reason why the door in the wall had suddenly clicked open. A faulty catch? Thoughts swirled through my exhausted yet fertile mind.

Sitting up in bed, watching the fire and the smoke curling up the chimney, I was lulled into an almost sleeplike trance, but subconsciously I was listening—waiting. The loneliness of the room, with its many shadows, seemed to envelop me. The stony-faced gentleman in the portrait over the fireplace continued to stare down, and his eyes seemed all too real.

I must have dozed for some time, for I awakened to see that the candle beside me was sputtering and in another few seconds would be extinguished. Fearfully, I lit another from the flame and dug it down into the candleholder. The fire needed attention, and I threw more coal and a log on it. I searched in my valise for my Testament, then hurried back to bed with it. I felt safer beneath the blankets and sheets, as I had as a small child—almost convinced that no harm could come to me in the safety of my own bed. Opening the Testament at random, I nervously started to read it out loud, although I scarcely comprehended the familiar words. My attention remained fixed on the paneled wall. And although I dozed several times that night, I did not sleep.

I had never been more thankful to see the glimmer of dawn. And as the windows lightened my spirits began to lift, even though a shroud of fog lingered outside my window, and I could see no more than a few yards of the grounds. There was a brilliant border of flowers beneath my window, and curiosity took its place beside my fear.

My last candle was guttering when I heard a knock at the door. It was my maid, who introduced herself as she set down a large kettle of hot water.

"Good morning, Lady Charlotte. I trust you slept well."

If I had not been so exhausted, I would probably have been able to restrain my almost hysterical laugh. "As well as can be expected. What is your name?"

"Ellie, yer ladyship."

"Do I detect a London accent?" I asked with some relief.

"Yes. Me mother and father left there for Cornwall two years ago. I certainly miss the city, m'lady."

"I'm sure you do. I miss it quite dreadfully myself—and I've only been gone six days."

Ellie took one of my dresses to be pressed, saying she would be back with it in time for breakfast. Glancing in the mirror, I wondered how I would ever make myself presentable.

In the mirror, I caught sight of the oak chest with which I

had barricaded the paneling. It was still in place, but it seemed to have been pushed away by as much as four inches. Could I have failed to push it against the wall? Or had the door been opened? My heart pounded as I heaved the chest back into position.

I undressed and hastily carried out my ablutions, longing to be out of the frightening room as quickly as possible. I donned my dressing gown and brushed my hair—listening again for any sign of movement behind the paneling.

Ellie's knock on the door startled me, and sent my heart beating wildly again. Trying to appear composed, I called out, "Enter!"

The maid, whom I now took time to study, was a round-cheeked young woman with curly black hair. Lingering behind her ready smile was an air of sadness and I felt a sense of kinship with her. While she helped me into my blue silk, empire-line dress, I asked about her ill mother.

"Oh, I'm so sorry I could not be 'ere when you arrived, yer ladyship." She continued, "Well, me mother is still unwell, and the doctor wonders if it might be something serious. She 'as been given medicine, so we all 'ope it will 'elp 'er."

She sighed, as if there were nothing more to say, and finished fastening my dress. "Such a lovely dress, yer ladyship. And it looks especially lovely on you, if you'll pardon my being so forward."

I thanked her and was grateful once more that the period of mourning for my mother was now over. The black, oppressive dresses had been left at home, save for my riding habit—which normally was of that color. I had not wanted to greet the children in black, lest it remind them of their own sadness.

It was time to go downstairs for breakfast and my meeting with Lord Penross. Throwing a light wool stole around my shoulders, I was thankful to leave the somber room, which had felt like a prison to me. I hurried down the long gallery with Ellie. As we descended the staircase, I could smell the tantalizing aromas of breakfast, and these spurred me on even faster.

In the hall, Mrs. Dawson was chastising one of the maids. She stopped the virulent outburst upon seeing me and bobbed a quick curtsy, uttering a slightly embarrassed,

"Good morning, yer ladyship." I returned her greeting, feeling sorry for the young girl who had been the victim of Mrs. Dawson's acid tongue.

Ellie opened the door to the breakfast room for me, and as I entered I saw Lord Penross seated at a large round table in the bay window, deeply engrossed in a newspaper—seemingly unaware of my entrance.

During that instant, I took the opportunity to study him. He was strikingly attired in a blue-gray jacket with a high collar and a white silk cravat. Dark hair and heavy eyebrows gave him a brooding, handsome, unapproachable look. His long, lean legs—encased in white, clinging trousers and high, black leather riding boots—were stretched out before him.

Without looking up, he said irritably, "Don't just stand there, girl—can't you see I need more toast!"

"I'm sorry, Lord Penross, I have none to give you," I answered him lightly.

He looked up, surprised, and his dark, questioning eyes met mine. "Lady Charlotte?" He rose in apology. "Forgive me, I thought you were one of the servants. Please, do sit here."

He pulled out the chair next to his, all the time unabashedly staring at me. Then, realizing what he was doing, he apologized once more.

"I cannot get over how much you have changed! I remember the young girl I met twelve years ago at your aunt's— Lady Sanford's."

There was a fleeting look of intense admiration that turned to a moment of awkwardness for both of us. I had not remembered how tall he was, nor how strikingly handsome. He looked away and I glanced around the room, noticing the opulent furnishings. Much to my relief, the sunny, bright colors of the curtains and upholstery made a direct contrast to the somber room in which I had spent the night. An enormous mahogany sideboard was laden with silver-covered dishes and a large tea urn.

"Please, you must be hungry." Lord Penross indicated I should help myself. "Breakfast is informal here." Then a slight smile turned up the corners of his mouth. "However, if you require toast, I fear you will have to wait."

I rose and quickly took one of the glistening, Penross-crested, white plates and began to lift the lid of each dish. Deciding upon a light breakfast of eggs and tea—and later, possibly, toast—I returned to the table. By then, Lord Penross was reading the newspaper once more, which I now saw was the *London Times* —a breath of familiar air—and wondered if there was any news of the impending war in France. My brother, Stephen, was never far from my mind.

I tried to partake of my meal as quietly as possible, feeling awkward that Lord Penross was not giving me his full attention and at the same time wanting to ask him many questions.

The door flew open and an obviously nervous young maid burst on the scene, bearing a tray upon which was a large silver rack containing the missing toast.

"Beg pardon, m' Lord," she sputtered. "The kitchen's in a real tizzy, and cook says she's sorry ye've 'ad to wait, but a 'uge load of soot fell down the chimney and messed up the first lot of toast!"

She clumsily put the toast rack down on the table, and rushed toward the door, endeavoring to avoid any more conversation with Lord Penross.

"One minute!" he thundered. "Why are you here and where is Rogers?"

"I don't know, m' Lord. I'm just doin' what I was told." The maid's face was now a bright scarlet. Lord Penross dismissed her and she ran out of the room. The door's closing noisily behind her added to his annoyance.

There was another awkward silence.

"I trust you slept well," he finally managed to say, politely.

I thought, "if only you knew," but managed to say, "Considering I was overtired from the journey, I feel somewhat rested, thank you, Lord Penross."

I had considered telling him of my terrifying experience but thought better of it—I feared he might think me a hysterical young woman, incapable of caring for his children. Besides, in this cheerful room the events of the night before seemed strangely unreal. I was almost willing to believe I had imagined them.

Lord Penross put down the newspaper. "Forgive my being so distracted by the *Times,* but it is only delivered here from

London three times a week. I have much pressing business of which I must keep abreast."

"But of course, Lord Penross." I hesitated for a moment, then asked, "May I presume to ask if I could possibly read it when you have finished with it?"

Folding the newspaper, he said, "Of course, Lady Charlotte. I know you will feel rather isolated here, and news from London will be most welcome. I shall see that it is left for you in the hall." I thanked him, and he continued, "I am deeply indebted to you for coming to care for my children. I have been troubled about their welfare—ever since my wife . . ." His voice trailed off, and he looked away.

"I do understand. I hope that I can in some way be of help. Losing my own mother last year makes me realize the enormity of their loss—and yours, Lord Penross."

"Thank you." He gazed at me briefly. "I do want you to feel that this is your home, and I trust that you will be happy here."

I thanked him, thinking what a contradictory personality he seemed to have—one moment seemingly tender and understanding, the next irritable and rude. But I also sensed an inner sadness that could be the reason for this contradiction. I made a mental note to try to please him with the way I managed the children.

Hesitating for a moment, I asked, "Lord Penross, perhaps tonight I might be able to sleep nearer the children. I do not mind if all the repairs are not completely finished in the room you had designated for me . . ."

"Repairs?"

"Yes. Because of the storms, apparently the room was damaged. I slept in the east wing—in the Green Room—last night."

He glanced at me from beneath dark eyebrows—a look of shock and concern in his eyes. "I am sorry you were given that room. It has not been used for some time. You will most certainly not sleep there tonight."

The large gilt mantle clock struck the half-hour, and Lord Penross changed the subject rapidly. "Before the children come down to meet you, I would like to talk with you concerning them. They do have a governess who teaches reading, writing, etcetera, etcetera. But what they need is someone to whom they can feel close—I am away a great deal."

"In this regard, Lord Penross, I would deem it a privilege if they would be allowed to call me Aunt Charlotte."

"An excellent idea . . . !" He thought for a moment. "I would ask that you be responsible for their religious instruction—seeing that they attend church and are cognizant of all the teachings."

He said it with the air of one for whom faith is a social responsibility, not a personal solace. Yet my own doubts made me hesitant to judge in such a matter; I merely expressed my approval and told him I would be delighted to take over such a meaningful responsibility.

"I understand from your aunt that you are a talented musician."

"I enjoy playing the pianoforte and flute, Lord Penross."

"Also, that you are a gifted artist. I would appreciate your instilling in my children a love of music and of the arts."

Smiling, I replied, "There will be so many beautiful scenes to paint around here that I am sure we will never run out of inspiration."

"You are fluent in several languages?"

"Latin, French, and a smattering of German."

"Perhaps you could commence with a smattering of Latin and French, then." He smiled at me, and for a few seconds the sadness in his eyes seemed to flee.

With that, the door opened and in ran the children— followed by what must be the nurserymaid. The little boy, who I had been told was seven years of age, immediately went over to Lord Penross and leant against him, burying his head into his father's shoulder. Then he turned to look at me, and his sparkling, blue eyes lit up.

"Her hair is just like Mama's was—the color of sunshine! That's what you used to say, Papa. It's the color of my hair, too." With that, he pulled a lock of his curls down to his nose and tried to see it.

"Yes, yes, William," Lord Penross interjected hastily, and dismissed the nurserymaid. "But let me introduce Lady Charlotte to you and your sister . . ."

The young girl—a beautiful twelve-year-old—had been watching me with a stiff, disapproving countenance.

"Lady Charlotte, these are my children, Elizabeth and William."

The boy ran over and took my hand, saying, "I've been looking forward to meeting you, Lady Charlotte. Will you please take me riding on my pony this afternoon?"

"It will be a pleasure—that is, if your father approves, William."

I looked into this beautiful child's face and felt an instant affinity and love. He had accepted me completely. But his sister was a different matter. She was a lovely child, having inherited her father's dramatic dark hair and eyes. But those eyes were filled with a burning resentment toward me.

"Lady Charlotte would like you to call her *Aunt* Charlotte, children, and I think it is a splendid idea." Lord Penross's tone of voice denoted that there was to be complete acceptance.

"Oh, yes," William piped up, "I shall love calling you Aunt Charlotte."

There was dead silence from Elizabeth, and then, in a voice that was barely audible, she said, "And I shall call you . . . Lady Charlotte."

4

*T*he coldness with which I was greeted by Elizabeth was repeated by her governess, Miss Marsden—a tall, thin, severe woman in her mid-forties. I met her when William insisted he show me the nursery and his bedroom. It was Saturday, and therefore there were no set lessons for him or Elizabeth.

The nursery was a bright room, although in need of refurbishing. A large table in the center of the room was covered by a heavy tapestry, upon which had been laid a smaller white linen tablecloth—already set for the children's lunch. A golden birdcage hung in the window, housing two bright yellow canaries, which hopped purposefully on their perches and twittered cheerfully. In front of the window was a large sofa, where dolls and toy soldiers were lined up in readiness for play. Skipping ropes hung neatly from brackets on the wall.

I peered out of the window, hoping that the fog had lifted and I could see what lay outside the walls of Penross. But the dense mist still hung opaquely before me.

Miss Marsden greeted me with the coldest "Good morning," I had ever encountered. The tightly drawn-back hair and her equally tight, thin mouth prophesied that my relationship with her would not be a happy one. I wondered why Lord Penross had allowed such an obviously unhappy woman to tutor his children.

Elizabeth ran to Miss Marsden and stood by her side—as if telling me where her loyalty would lie. William, on the other hand, kept taking my hand, delighted to be showing me all his treasures.

"Come see my bedroom, Aunt Charlotte . . ."

I saw a fleeting, questioning expression on Miss Marsden's face. "The children are to call you Aunt Charlotte?" she asked stiffly.

"If they wish to, yes, Miss Marşden."

Elizabeth stared at me, then turned to Miss Marsden. "I wish to call her Lady Charlotte."

"That is perfectly all right with me, Elizabeth," I said. "I just want you to know that my being here will in no way interfere with your lessons with Miss Marsden. I look forward to our learning about music, art, and languages."

Even though I addressed myself to Elizabeth, my main purpose was to make Miss Marsden understand I would not be encroaching on her territory in any way.

"Come, see my bedroom!" William pulled me toward his door. It was a rather bleak room with a small, spartan bed near the window. Perhaps later I would be able to furnish it with some bright pictures. A large rocking horse dominated the center of the room.

"That's Marengo—I named it after Napoleon's horse, because one day he'll be mine when we defeat old Boney Bonaparte for good!" William jumped up and down on his bed—much to the chagrin of Miss Marsden, who had followed behind me.

"Master William, you know that is not allowed. Get down immediately!" The harshness in her voice caused William to stop his jumping, and his smile of triumph vanished.

"At this time on Saturday, the children engage in making toys for the poor children of the village, Lady Charlotte." Miss Marsden was clearly trying to be rid of me, and I gladly left the nursery, with a promise to William that we would go riding later in the day if the weather cleared.

Across the corridor from the nursery, the door to a bed-chamber was wide open, and I saw that my trunks had been delivered there. I put my head around the door—no one was present. My valises had been unpacked, and I saw that my personal effects were now ensconced—making it seem a trifle more like home. My mother's brass carriage clock now graced the mantlepiece. The leather-bound volume of the latest Jane Austen novel, *Mansfield Park,* bought for me by Stephen as a going-away present, was on the table by my bed. Beside it were miniatures of my parents and of Stephen in his Coldstream Guards' uniform.

It was a beautiful room, furnished comfortably as a bed-room and sitting room with a chaise lounge, an armchair and footstool, and other delicate furniture that reminded me of my bedroom in London. The bed hangings and cur-tains were of a pale yellow damask that made the room seem as if the sun were shining even on such a dark, misty morn-ing. Richly colored oriental rugs warmed the highly polished parquet flooring and added to the feeling of comfort. There were two large windows; one faced south to the sea, and the other to the west. A window seat stretched across the bay window facing the sea—I knew this would be my special haven.

The fire burning merrily in the grate gave the room an even cozier feeling. Thoughts of immediately returning to London were beginning to fade. The manor was beautiful. My room was warm. And William was such a delightful child; I knew the days ahead could be happy ones in his innocently mischievous company.

Elizabeth, of course, would be a challenge. I would have to earn her respect. In a way, I understood how she must be feeling—possibly that I had come to usurp her mother's memory. It would be a delicate tightrope I would tread—and not only with her, but with the forbidding Miss Marsden.

The fog was finally beginning to lift, and directly below my window I could now see a colorful, formal Italian sunken garden. Statuary and precisely cut privet hedges bordered the mass of brilliant flowers. Beyond it I could almost make out the edge of the cliff upon which Penross stood—and beyond it, the sea. I could hear it thundering against the rocks, and I remembered the breathtakingly beautiful view of the mansion and cliffs illuminated by a flash of lightning.

A path led to a walkway along the edge; I hastily found my hunter-green wool cape and flung it over my shoulders, a shiver of excitement running through me. I had once been to the seaside at Brighton—when my parents were invited to stay by the Prince Regent—but the tame, pebbly beach there could not compare with the splendid grandeur of the Cornish coastline. I wanted to explore.

Passing by the other window on my way to the door, I could now see the western view. The coastline twisted and turned into the distance, revealing many small coves and one large one guarded by giant, menacing, monolithic rocks. Lush green grass led down to the the brink of the cliffs, punctuated by some of the most oddly contorted trees I had ever seen. I tied my cape more tightly around me and wanted to run down the corridor, but decorum did not permit it. Instead, I walked with the dignity befitting my new status. "Aunt Charlotte" proceeded down the staircase, head erect— trying not to betray the excitement welling within her.

Rogers, the butler, was standing in the hallway, in the process of placing several envelopes upon a silver salver. His back was toward me, and when I greeted him he straightened and turned—startled—to look at me.

"Lady Charlotte! Ah, I see you have a letter. . . . I trust it bears good news."

He handed it to me, and I realized he had been about to investigate from whom it came. I felt his eyes follow me as I thanked him for it and proceeded to walk out the front door.

The wind coming straight from the sea caught me off guard, but the bracing air was welcome after the somewhat stifling, yet chilly, atmosphere in the great house. Walking along the path that led to the cliffs, I felt free. The wind whipped my hair across my eyes, and I pushed it back whilst looking at the envelope. It was from Stephen, of course. I saved it to read once I was out of sight from the house and could find a sheltered spot.

As I approached the edge of the cliff, something made me look back at Penross Manor. Again I was struck by the magnificence of its architecture. But as I stood gazing at the noble structure of brick, stone, and timber, my eyes kept returning to the window high in the eastern turret where I thought I had seen a man. I could see nothing now. Again I wondered—could it have been Lord Penross? Would the lightning have made him seem so menacing?

I turned away and proceeded to walk along the cliff's edge, looking down at the relentless surf as it crashed against the rocks and left a sparkling white spray. Seagulls weaved and maneuvered perilously in search of food—their cries a cacophony of discordant sound that mixed with the sea's own thunderous voice.

Rounding a corner, I found a sheltered gazebo and gladly stepped up into its white, dome-like structure. A solitary bench was its only furnishing; I sat down and tore open the seal of my letter from Stephen, eagerly reading the familiar handwriting. The last two paragraphs brought tears to my eyes:

. . . This may be my last letter to you for a while. With Napoleon's escape from Elba, the regiment is ready to leave at a moment's notice. I do not know what lies ahead for me, but the promise of your prayers and the knowledge that I shall not go into battle alone—Almighty God will be with me—give me courage. Do not be afraid for me, sister, dear.

Now we are parted by so many miles, but may the year see the end of any new threat of invasion by France, so that all England may rejoice and live in peace—and you and I will be reunited. Until then, I shall not cease to thank our Lord for all your love and understanding.

Your affectionate brother,
Stephen

I buried my head into my hands and cried for all the love we had for each other. Then, leaving the gazebo, I looked eastward in the direction where Stephen must be and silently—almost out of habit—asked the Lord to be with him. "He's all I have left, Heavenly Father." My feeling of desolation did not go away.

Gathering my cloak around me, I continued to walk westward along the rim of the cliff. "A sudden gale could sweep me down upon the rocks," I thought, and edged away from the mesmerizing height that was at once frightening and beautiful.

I came to several small coves that would be inviting to explore when the weather became warmer. Then, just ahead of me, I saw a large cove that must have been the one I had seen from my bedroom window. The giant, jagged rocks protruded from the golden sands, strewn with seaweed and the enormous wrecked hulls of many ships that had come to grief in some prior, violent storms. Below me was an inlet that looked as if it led to a cave. A small rowboat was anchored nearby, and for an instant I saw two men deep in conversation. They then disappeared behind the rocks.

Their presence unnerved me, for I wondered how long they had been standing there and whether they had been watching me. I decided to walk back along the pathway and, deep in thought, watched a ship way out on the horizon.

The sound of horse's hoofs made me turn back to look at the house; Lord Penross was riding toward me. He dismounted from a gleaming black animal and, holding the reins, walked up to me, a disturbed expression upon his face.

"Lady Charlotte, I should have warned you that Tregoran Cove is forbidden to the children, and I trust you will not go near there again. Too many unfortunate incidents have taken place there, and I do not wish to see any harm come to you."

His penetrating, deep-brown eyes searched mine, and once more I felt a disturbing attraction between us. There was something magnetic about his presence . . .

Turning from him, so that he could not see that the color in my cheeks had heightened, I said, "I thank you, Lord Penross, for your warning. It is strange, but even having no prior knowledge of the cove, I sensed that it was an unhappy place. Then, when I saw the wrecks of those ships, I knew what sorrow must have been experienced there."

Lord Penross walked with me, his head down. "Indeed, there have been many wrecks—most of them planned."

"I do not understand, Lord Penross. Do you mean the crews deliberately wrecked their ships?" I asked incredulously.

"No. Many were lured there by men—and sometimes women—with lanterns. During storms, sailors, desperate to see the lights of land, thought it was a safe harbor." He paused, as if not wanting to give me any more of the grisly details. Then he continued, "The 'wreckers,' as they are called, would wait until morning—at which time they killed any poor souls who had survived the shipwreck and stripped them of all their belongings, stealing whatever they could of the ship's cargo."

"How terrible!" I cried. The wind whipped the words from

my mouth and I turned to face Lord Penross. "Does this still go on, even today?"

"Yes, in spite of the fact that the King's preventive men try to patrol the coastline. It is not a part of Cornish history of which I am proud, Lady Charlotte. That is why I have forbidden the children to go near the sea unless I accompany them."

I remembered the two men I had seen in the cove. Could it be they were plotting a "wrecking"?

Lord Penross's voice interrupted my thoughts. "I trust I have not upset you, Lady Charlotte. It is best, though, that you are familiar with what goes on in this part of England." He changed his expression. "Come, let me show you the horse that is at your disposal. I have chosen him for you myself. His name is Guardian—and I trust he will be just that to you."

I walked with Lord Penross to the stables and, upon seeing the magnificent chestnut horse, thanked my host for such a fine mount.

"I look forward to riding him with William, Lord Penross."

He gazed down at me, a smile curling his lips. "I trust I shall have the honor of your allowing me to accompany you also, Lady Charlotte."

"It will be a pleasure . . ." I whispered.

5

Disconcerted by Lord Penross's attention toward me, I suggested that the groom be sent to fetch William, so that the child could enjoy a ride on his pony before luncheon. The man was hastily dispatched, and Lord Penross took the opportunity to point out the local scenery and landmarks to me.

The fog had completely disappeared, and I could now see for miles. The wild Cornish moors, with their scattered granite rocks, lay to the north—stretching as far east and west as the eye could see. Richly wooded hills of mighty oaks, elms, and firs framed the imposing Penross Manor, gleaming splendidly in the late morning sunshine. The small fishing village of Penross lay below us to the west, and I could now see the boats moored in the harbor—their sails fluttering like proud pennants in the brisk sea breeze.

"The town you see in the distance, Lady Charlotte, is Falmouth—one of our most prominent ports. It was from there that England first heard of Lord Nelson's victory at Trafalgar. HMS *Pickles* brought the dispatch, and it was taken by mail coach to London."

"Oh, I remember when we got the news—people were celebrating in the streets!" I smiled, thinking of that incredible day, then added—as I stopped to take in the panoramic scene of the waterfront before me—"I am amazed to see so many ships and—"

"Wait until you see the fishing boats at night, Aunt Charlotte! Their lanterns look like glowworms out at sea!"

I turned to see William running excitedly in front of the groom and extended my hand in welcome. William took it and immediately began to lead me toward his gentle, piebald pony, which had now been saddled.

"Isn't he the finest pony you've ever seen?"

"Undoubtedly, William. Among all those that I've encountered in Hyde Park, in London, there's not been a finer one." We laughed together as he mounted the small, docile animal.

"Watch me, Papa, I can jump him now. Harris taught me while you were away last time."

Lord Penross immediately restrained the pony by grabbing hold of the reins. "William, it is far too dangerous for you to jump around here. Remember what I told you about the ha-ha ditches." Lord Penross turned toward me. "Forgive me for sounding so stern, but they are very dangerous."

"What is a 'ha-ha'—and what are they for?" I asked, bewildered. I felt very much the Londoner, ignorant in matters pertaining to the countryside.

"They were invented during the last century by William Kent so that the garden could merge with the landscape— thus making fences or hedges unnecessary, as deer and cattle will not venture over them. The name originated when riders came upon them unexpectedly and uttered an expression of surprise." We laughed together at the thought. Then Lord Penross became serious. "I sometimes think I should have them all filled in, however, as they can be perilous to unsuspecting riders."

"I shall be most careful, Lord Penross, and so will William, will you not?" The boy reluctantly nodded his head and told his father he would not jump anymore unless he was told he could. He was satisfied to show me the gardens from his mount, pointing out the different birds and flowers that grew so abundantly. I walked beside him, marveling at the beauty. I had heard the sea air produced magnificent foliage and plants. Before me, wherever I looked in the parkland surrounding Penross Manor, the landscape was a perfect example.

Lord Penross suggested we all go for a short ride, but I

was not suitably attired. "I shall have to wait for our ride together, Lord Penross. I do not wish to keep you waiting while I change into my riding habit. William will be pleased to have you to himself for a while, I am sure."

"Very well, Lady Charlotte. We will meet again at luncheon."

Lord Penross led his horse past the carriage house, and shouted to the coachman, who was repairing a wheel.

"Will that be ready by two o'clock? I expect to leave for Exeter on time, Trigg."

"You will, m'lord. It buckled in the storm last night, due to the ruts in the road." Trigg glowered at me as if it were my fault. His eyes still bore the contemptuous look he had bestowed on me the day he arrived at my house in London.

So Lord Penross would be leaving with him this afternoon. I wondered how long he would be away. It would seem strange to be without his company in this great house so soon—unsure of my duties and the environs.

Lord Penross proceeded out of the courtyard on horseback, followed by William. "Luncheon will be at one o'clock, Lady Charlotte. But perhaps you would like me to show you some of the house before then?"

"I would, indeed."

"Then let us meet in the hall at noon."

I nodded my assent and watched as Lord Penross and William began their ride together. The little boy turned and waved, a smile lighting up his sunny face. Then they disappeared under the archway leading out to the park, and I began to walk slowly back toward Penross Manor.

Last night, I could see the great house was large, but broad daylight revealed quite a few wings I had not been aware of. The great Elizabethan house must have been added to over the centuries, for I could see the influence of many different types of architecture. I looked forward to learning more of the history of this magnificent mansion.

And yet I was disturbed by a feeling of being watched; it seemed every window was an eye looking down at me. In the shadows of each room, I felt as if someone were watching.

Perhaps it was simply the size of the place, the echoing silence of its halls. Yet my family's house in the country had been quite large, and I had never sensed any kind of ominous feelings the whole time I had lived there. In fact, the atmosphere had been one of great joy and relaxation. I remember guests often remarked about the sense of well-being and contentment that emanated from its walls—no doubt due, in many ways, to the love my parents had for one another and for their children.

In the distance, church bells were chiming the hour—I counted to eleven. With an hour left before I was to meet Lord Penross, I decided to walk to the back of the great house and explore the territory there. Gorse-covered moors made the landscape look as if the sun were forever shining, and I walked for several miles—at times finding difficulty in walking over the granite rocks that scarred the rugged land.

Upon returning to the manor, I noticed a small private chapel that extended north from the west wing. It looked as if it had not been used for some time. Hesitantly, I tried the latch. The door was unlocked, although the hinges groaned as I pushed against it. And then, there before me—the sunlight streaming through the stained glass windows to leave a pool of multicolored light upon the altar—was a darkly paneled, subdued, Elizabethan place of worship.

I slowly walked down the aisle, feeling as if I were intruding upon someone's personal retreat. An atmosphere of uncanny quiet pervaded. There were brass and slate memorials to Lord Penross's ancestors lining the walls on either side of the aisle—some dating back to the seventeenth century. Then I noticed a new, more elaborate, white marble one near the altar:

In loving memory of my beautiful wife, Caroline,
who departed this life the fifteenth of March,
in the year of our Lord, eighteen hundred and thirteen.

Lady Caroline Penross—devoted wife,
and mother of William and Elizabeth—
aged twenty eight years.

"Ever with the Lord."

I thought that soon it would be two years since Lady Penross had died. And she had been so young—only two years older than I was now . . .

A small brass vase containing primroses and bluebells had been placed by the memorial. The manner in which they had been arranged caused me to think that one of the children had left them there.

I felt once more as if I were intruding, and turned to leave. A door near the altar was slightly ajar, and I wondered where it led—possibly back to the main house. I walked toward it, at the same time looking at Lady Penross's memorial, and wondering how she had died. My aunt had seemed vague when I had asked her, but perhaps Ellie would know.

Near the open door by the altar was a framed letter from King Charles II—thanking an earlier Lord Penross for his assistance during the Great Civil War almost two centuries before. I remembered that Cornwall had played an important part in the war between the Royalists and Cromwell's men, and I wondered just what assistance the Penrosses had given . . .

With a final glance back at Lady Penross's memorial, I left the chapel by way of the altar door. My heart felt heavy, indeed, as I thought of all the sorrow that had been experienced by Lord Penross and the children.

I found myself in a long, dusty corridor lined with white marble statues on either side—their sightless eyes staring into space. I hurried past them, hoping to find a way back to the inhabited part of the house. The lofty windows in the corridor looked out onto a dark, unkempt courtyard, and from the other side I saw equally dark windows staring back at me. I approached the end of the corridor and a door that I hoped was not locked. The brass knob turned in my hand and I was thankful to find myself now in a brighter corridor leading to the main hall. Lord Penross was pacing up and down, waiting for me.

"Forgive me, I did not mean to keep you waiting."

He smiled, somewhat distantly. "You are only a few minutes late, Lady Charlotte. Have you been exploring on your own?"

I hesitated to say where I had been, yet did not want to appear secretive. "Yes, Lord Penross. I came upon the chapel. It's very beautiful."

His face clouded over. "We do not use it now for services. The parish church close to the main gates is where we worship. You will be attending there tomorrow, with the children."

"Oh, yes, I remember seeing it as I drove by last night."

There was an awkward silence. Then Lord Penross said, briskly, "Let me show you where the main rooms are." He walked ahead of me, pointing out different rooms but not stopping, and I found it difficult to keep up with him. The drawing-room doors were open, and he paused for a moment. "This room you will find to be most comfortable, Lady Charlotte. As you can see, the windows command a delightful view."

It was a particularly charming room, furnished in a relaxed manner. The oil paintings were of landscapes and horses—a pleasing change from the formal family portraits that seemed to haunt me wherever I went. I would have liked to linger there, but Lord Penross continued to walk briskly down a long dark corridor. He came to some massive dark oak doors and flung them open.

"This is the library. You will find many rare books here, and I trust you will feel at liberty to use them."

I thanked him and looked around the vast room, its walls completely covered—except for the windows, which looked out to the sea—with the most incredible collection of leather-bound books of varying hues. On the spines were many familiar names—Donne, Pepys, Dr. Johnson, Wordsworth . . .

"I believe this is one of the most comprehensive collections in the country. Anything you wish to study can be found here. I would like you to read to the children often, Lady Charlotte."

"It will be my privilege to share the wonder of literature with Elizabeth and William, Lord Penross. It has afforded me many hours of great pleasure."

I looked over at a small, beautifully carved table next to a lady's upholstered chair, and saw a book lying open—its pages adorned by a bright-green silk bookmark.

"Why, it's Jane Austen's *Pride and Prejudice!* How I enjoy her books," and I proceeded to walk toward it.

"No, do not touch it," Lord Penross thundered, and his voice startled me. I stood rooted to the spot—not knowing what I had done to offend him. Then his mood changed to one of great remorse.

"Forgive me, Lady Charlotte, forgive me." He walked over to the open book and peered down at it. "My wife was reading this the day she died. I have left strict instructions to the servants never to move it."

I began an apology, but he raised his hand to silence me. "It is I who must apologize." Then, impulsively, he picked up the book and deliberately shut it. Then he handed it to me. "Please—take this. I want you to have it—Caroline would have wanted me to give it to someone who would appreciate it."

"Lord Penross, I cannot accept it. Your daughter, Elizabeth, should be given her mother's book."

"She has been given many of her possessions. I would like you to have the book. There—that is final. Please do not mention it again." His tone of voice commanded that there be no more argument. "Come, let me show you the music room. You will spend many happy hours there, I am sure."

I followed him, clutching the book and feeling most awkward concerning it. He strode on down another corridor and ushered me into the music room.

It was a bright, majestic room with mirrored walls. Ornate chandeliers hung from the ceiling, and I could imagine days in the past when recitals would have been given there. In the corner, near the great bay window, was a superb pianoforte. My eyes lit up as I walked toward it—never had I seen a finer instrument.

"Play something for me, Lady Charlotte. I can see you appreciate the beauty of the pianoforte."

"Indeed, oh, yes, indeed!" I walked over and carefully laid down the book by Jane Austen on top of the highly polished satinwood. Sitting down, I paused for a moment, looking at the magnificent keyboard, and then began to play a sonata by Haydn—the beauty of the surroundings seeming to be in harmony with the composer's mood when he had written the haunting melody.

For a few moments I became unaware of my surroundings, and was lost in the balance and serenity of Haydn's music. As the last note of the movement was played, there was a silence—then Lord Penross clapped his hands.

"Magnificent, Lady Charlotte. You are indeed a gifted pianist. I have not heard Haydn played so movingly."

He came over and leaned over the curve of the piano, looking down at me with admiration.

I blushed, sensing once more his regard for me. After whispering, "thank you," I quickly began to play Bach—leading into one of his church preludes and finally, "Jesu, Joy of Man's Desiring."

At the end, Lord Penross said, in hushed tones, "I can tell that work means a great deal to you."

"It does." Tears were not far away. "I played this often after my mother died, and each time sensed the Lord's comfort."

"I shall have to ask you to play it frequently." His eyes were hooded with sorrow, and he turned away from me and walked to the door. "We must not be late for luncheon. I leave for Exeter in an hour."

His mood had changed rapidly, and I sensed he did not wish to dwell on the past.

As we walked into the dining hall, I asked if he would be away for some time. "Only two nights, it is to be hoped," he replied, ushering me to a chair near to his at the head of the long, highly polished table.

The room was vast, and I felt chilled sitting at the great table, empty save for the enormous gilt centerpiece and two place settings. The highback chairs seemed like silent, disapproving sentinels, and the portraits and tapestries—together with warlike battle-axes, pistols, spears, and swords hanging on the great high walls—did nothing to soften the forbidding atmosphere. Over the great stone fireplace was the now-familiar crest of the Penross family—an arm, clad in armor and brandishing a sword, upraised in the center of a shield. I looked up to see that a minstrel gallery ran high along the northern end of the room—most of it cloaked in shadows.

Sensing my dislike of the room, Lord Penross laughed. "It is a large room for just two of us, is it not? Tradition has always been that when a Penross is in residence here, the dining room is used for both luncheon and dinner. I would sooner use the breakfast room for all my meals, but Rogers insists it is no more work for him or the other servants for me to eat here and carry on the tradition. Is that not so, Rogers?"

The butler had entered the room and was quietly in-structing Tom—the young footman who had been so help-ful last night—to leave a great tureen on the sideboard.

"Yes, m'lord. Your father would have wished you to carry on the tradition." Unsmilingly, he served a large bowl of soup to me, and I wondered how I would ever eat the rest of the meal. Now the sideboard was beginning to be laden with many elaborate, covered dishes.

Catching my look of apprehension, Lord Penross laughed once more. "Rogers, we will have to see that Lady Charlotte is given smaller portions."

Rogers glared at me, then smiled as Lord Penross turned to him. "But of course, m'lord . . ." I wondered how I was going to endure the loneliness of meals served by such an obviously hostile servant. Trying to give the impression I was enjoying my luncheon, I nevertheless picked at the rest of the meal.

As soon as dessert was finished, Lord Penross excused himself to take leave of the children. In the hall, his luggage was being carried out—it seemed a great deal for just two nights away. Although I had only met Lord Penross that morning, and he was a man of obviously diverse and some-times explosive moods, I felt as if a friend was leaving me alone in this great house.

"Have a safe trip, Lord Penross," I told him as he re-turned from the nursery. "I will see that the children are well cared for—in fact, perhaps this afternoon we can begin some artwork. William has expressed to me his de-sire to paint a scene of the fishing boats . . ." I knew my voice had a note of nervousness, and Lord Penross was quick to notice.

His hand briefly touched my shoulder as if in reassur-ance. "I know you will be most attentive to the children. I leave them in your most capable hands."

The housekeeper, Mrs. Dawson, who had been standing in the background, exchanged glances with Rogers, and I saw her chin go up defiantly. I realized that if I were ever to be comfortable in this house I would have to move now and establish some authority.

"Thank you, Lord Penross, for your trust in me." My

voice was now a tone louder—to let the servants hearing it know I was not to be underestimated.

Rogers helped Lord Penross on with his black-caped greatcoat and handed him a silver-buckled, tall-crowned hat. Quickly, Lord Penross gripped my hand and bade me farewell.

Trigg was standing by the coach and opened the door as soon as he saw Lord Penross emerge. He doffed his hat and bowed slightly. "We should make Exeter in good time, m'lord."

"See that you do, Trigg."

Each time I saw the coachman he reminded me of a sly, unkempt black raven—his beady eyes always traveling to and fro, afraid of missing some delectable morsel . . .

Lord Penross entered the coach, then pulled down the window and waved goodbye to me. His eyes held mine until the coach moved, and then he was gone—leaving me standing on the steps of Penross Manor, alone. I watched the coach descending down the long, tree-lined driveway until it was out of sight.

I sensed once more the vastness of the great estate. A feeling of loneliness swept over me and I longed for the familiar streets of London.

Back inside the house, I walked past Rogers and Mrs. Dawson. Lord Penross had left the *Times* for me in the hall. Taking it, I proceeded to the foot of the stairs before I delivered the little speech I had been rehearsing silently for the past ten minutes:

"I shall have tea at four o'clock, with the children in the nursery, Rogers. No, on second thought, I would like it served in my room."

As I walked up the stairs, I could sense his and Mrs. Dawson's eyes on me.

"It is the usual practice at Penross for Miss Marsden to have tea with the children, m'lady," Rogers answered with a note of disparagement.

"From now on, Rogers, I intend often to have tea with the children—regardless of the past."

My hands were trembling as I gripped the balustrade, but I did not look back. I prayed that they would not know how alarmed I felt concerning them—and concerning this forever brooding, somber house.

6

A bright, soulful moon bathed Penross and the ever- changing sea in a brilliant wash of light. The sunken Italian gardens took on a new dimension because of the eerie shadows cast by statuary and shrubs. Looking at the small maze from the height of my window, I could now see that it was easily solved. I would have to remember, next time William gave me only two minutes to extricate myself from the confusing warren of high privet hedges.

This afternoon, after his first lesson in painting, William had dared me to find my way out of the intricate maze, and I had finally had to call him for help.

Reclining on the window seat, I could see the "glowworms" my new little friend had told me about—the lights from the fishing fleet danced and bobbed on the horizon. No doubt the fishermen were taking advantage of the fine weather and hoping for a good catch. Many of the villagers' livelihoods were tied to the benevolence of the fickle sea. And I had been told their fish-cellars were almost empty because of the violent storms during the last weeks.

There was so much to learn about the rugged life of the Cornish people. Although we were of the same nation, I felt a foreigner amongst them. I did know, however, that their whole way of life had been threatened by Napoleon's fanatical ambition to rule the world. So many of the families had suffered either from the loss of loved ones or from having them return dreadfully wounded and unable to be providers. Of course, this was true in London and all over England, and I myself knew the pain of separation. But the tragedy had been brought home to me in a more direct way when I heard firsthand from Ellie, my maid, of the hardships that were taking place in the village and, only a few miles away, in the port of Falmouth. I would have to ask the vicar what could be done to help these people. There would be much idle time for me—once the children were in bed, my evenings would be lonely indeed, especially if Lord Penross were to be away so often.

I wrapped my dressing gown closer around me, drawing my knees up beneath my chin, and leant my head against the window frame. Dinner had been a grim affair—I had sat alone in the great dining hall, served by the ever-rigid, unfathomable Rogers. I had felt an unwelcome outsider, and the family portraits had seemed to glare down from their gilded frames, disdain written upon their noble faces. I would ask Lord Penross to allow me to take my meals in my room whenever he was away.

However, tea had been a disaster here. It had started with a defiant Miss Marsden telling me I had no right to change the children's schedule and refusing to join me. Then Elizabeth had sat by the fire, angrily saying that this would always be her mother's sitting room as far as she was concerned. My presence in it was not welcome, and she would speak to her father upon his return.

As I was offering William a dish of cakes to choose from, a gasp of surprise and indignant concern had escaped Elizabeth. She had jumped up and run over to the small escritoire, where I had left her mother's book. Snatching up *Pride and Prejudice,* she had angrily asked who had given permission for me to bring it to my room.

"Your father, Elizabeth. I would not have dreamed to be so presumptuous otherwise."

"It had been left exactly as Mama was reading it . . ." Her impassioned anger had spilled over into tears, and I was reminded of her father once more. "We were never, ever going to touch it!" She clutched the book to her.

I could not bring myself to tell her that Lord Penross had

actually given it to me. "I will see that it is put back, Elizabeth."

"No, *I* shall put it back!" And with a look of hatred toward me, she had run out of the room.

William had been disturbed by her outburst and had come over to me. "I'm glad you are in Mama's sitting room. It's been so lonely to open the door of the nursery, and look across the hall, and only see an empty room. Mama used to read to us here every day." Looking up at me, his eyes brimming with tears, he said, "I still miss her, Aunt Charlotte."

"I know you must, William." My arms had gone around this vulnerable child, and I prayed that somehow I could help alleviate the sorrow he had experienced so young.

"God is watching over you—and your mother. He loves you both very much."

The tender, blue eyes had looked into mine. "If He does, then why did He let my mother die, Aunt Charlotte?"

"I don't know, William. We can't understand all that God allows—but we do know that in time it will be made clear to us. You see, this life is really only a beginning—there's so much more to come. One day we are going to see all those who have gone before us and are with God."

I had been reassuring myself as much as William. The stark, comfortless memory of my own mother's funeral had almost destroyed any expectations of being reunited.

"Well, I would just like to be with Mama *now*." William had walked over to the door, "I just don't think God is very fair, Aunt Charlotte." He had started to go out of the room, then hesitated for a minute. "But I'm glad He sent you here."

Running back to me, he had put his arms around my neck and given me a tight hug—which I returned. "Thank you. I'm so glad I've come to know you, William." And then we had sat talking for quite some time. Only when the fire had begun to sink lower in the grate had I realized it was a long time since tea, and close to a seven-year-old's bedtime. "Now, why don't you get ready for bed, and I'll come and read you a story before you say your prayers?"

The time I had spent with William had made me feel my long journey from London was worthwhile. I could see how hungry the child was for someone who cared for him, who would take the time to make him feel loved. His relationship with his father seemed forever fleeting—Lord Penross was obviously a man who could not take the time that was necessary for so young a child. Of course, the pressures of running such a vast estate cut deeply into his days. But I wondered, even if Lord Penross had the time, whether he was the type of person to spend it with a seven-year-old.

Elizabeth had not returned after her angry outburst, and I found myself wondering whether she would ever come to trust me. I felt hurt by Elizabeth's unreasonable outburst toward me—yet I could not help but understand. The lonely lives the children led, with such a cold, unbending governess, caused me to perceive all the pent-up emotion the young girl must feel.

Glancing over at the carriage clock, I saw it was past eleven o'clock. Sleep continued to evade me. I got up from the window seat and restlessly began to pace up and down the room. I should have to get used to evenings that had so many solitary hours.

This night I could not seem to concentrate on the Jane Austen book Stephen had given to me. Perhaps reading my Testament would give me a sense of peace that was missing. I could not remember a night when I had forgotten to read from it—even last night, when I had been so frightened.

But the little Book was not on the bed table. Perhaps Ellie had put it in the drawer—no, it was not there either. I searched the room, but without success. Even a quick look through a trunk not yet unpacked failed to reveal the missing Testament.

Then, I remembered . . . this morning, in the Green Room, I had placed it in the drawer of the table by the bed and had forgotten to retrieve it before leaving the frightening room. I would have to wait until morning before asking Ellie to get it for me.

The thought crossed my mind that I should go—right now—and find it. If I were to stay in this great house I would have to learn not to be afraid of it. I must take hold of my far-too-active imagination and put aside the fears that so often assailed me.

I opened the door to my room and looked out down the

long hallway to the east wing. The candles had been extinguished, but I would not need their light, nor need I take the candelabrum brightly burning by my bedside. Moonlight spilled through the long windows, illuminating the way for me.

I would have to pass the suits of armor, which flanked the walls—mysteriously silent, as if waiting once more to be used in battle. Stephen had known of my fear of the ones in our house in the country when we were children, and he had delighted in telling me that there were really still men inside—peering through the visors in their helmets, waiting to pounce on me as I passed by.

"Go on, Charlotte, open the visors and see their eyes looking back at you . . ." I had run from them, terrified that they would come after me.

These childish fears returned as I began the long walk to the Green Room. A chill went down my spine when I was halfway down the wide corridor. The moonlight made the suits of armor gleam, and from out of the corner of my eye I thought I saw them move.

"You are so foolish, Charlotte," I told myself. A vivid imagination could be a great disadvantage. There were no men inside the armor, and it was impossible for them to move . . . I would have to share my ridiculous imaginings with William tomorrow.

Approaching the Green Room, I hoped that the door was not locked—as it had been upon my arrival last night. The latch turned and I quickly entered, not wanting to spend one more second than necessary in the terrifying room. I walked over to the nightstand and opened the drawer, and there, in the moonlight, I saw my Testament.

My hand was reaching out for it when I thought I heard a sound. Turning quickly, I looked toward the window and saw—silhouetted against the moonlight—the figure of a man. I felt my mouth go dry and my throat constrict. The man's back was toward me, and he did not move. I wondered if he had heard me come into the room. Then he turned slightly and relief swept over me.

"Forgive me, Lord Penross," I said in a voice that shook from fright, and then relief. "I did not realize you had returned; I would have knocked before entering. My Testament was left here, and I wished to read it before retiring for the night. Please, do excuse me."

He raised his right hand as if in acquiescence, but did not turn to me. I picked up my Testament and left the room hastily, closing the door behind me, then walked swiftly back to my room—its warm environs being most welcome.

It was evident that Lord Penross had changed his plans and returned this evening; he could not possibly have gone to Exeter and back in the time. I wondered what could have happened. It was good to know that he was in the house once more, and I felt a renewed sense of well-being. For a few minutes I read my Testament, and after a prayer I blew out the candles and settled down in bed. My eyes were beginning to feel heavy now, and I knew that sleep would not be far off.

Drowsily, I wondered why Lord Penross had gone to the lonely Green Room. He had reacted so negatively at breakfast when I had told him that I had spent last night there. What was it about that room that held unpleasant associations for him?

I looked around my own room, thankful for the familiar objects that I had brought from home. The miniatures of my parents and Stephen were on the table by the bed, and a shaft of moonlight made them plainly visible. I reached out and touched each one, praying that God would keep Stephen safe this night.

I had almost drifted off to sleep when I heard what seemed to be the rumbling of a coach, or maybe a cart, nearby. My room was the nearest to the stables, so perhaps someone was returning at this late hour. Or possibly Lord Penross's coach was being taken to the carriage house.

I got out of bed and walked over to the window, but could see nothing. Then I heard the noise again—a low rumbling that sounded as if it were caused by a well-laden conveyance. I would ask in the morning what it could possibly be. But now I must sleep. Seven o'clock would come soon enough.

I was about to climb back into bed when once more the memory of the man standing by the window flashed before me. I had presumed it to be Lord Penross, but now it seemed as if there had been something about the man that did not ring true. Why had he not turned to me when I spoke to him? I had taken for granted it was Lord Penross. But was there something different about that silhouette? Perhaps it had been one of the servants? No, the figure had been too well dressed—and taller than any of the servants I had met . . .

A feeling of cold terror ran through me . . . I might have been alone in that dark room with a stranger! And once more, in spite of myself, I envisioned the face in the turret window. Shaking, I walked swiftly to my bedchamber door, turned the key in the lock, and pushed the bolt in place.

7

Sunday morning, still shaken from my encounter of the night before, I stood in the hallway waiting for the children to come down. It was already ten minutes until eleven, and the church bells had begun to chime—calling the people of Penross village to worship. I had dressed warmly in my deep burgundy dress and matching bonnet, together with a heavy fur pelisse and muff. Ellie had warned me that the church would be painfully cold. However, there would be foot warmers already waiting for us in the family pew—for which I was most grateful.

Footsteps could be heard racing down the hallway above, and then William came charging down the stairs, still trying to fasten his overcoat.

"Where is Elizabeth?" I asked.

"She says she has a cold, Aunt Charlotte, and so does Miss Marsden." He whispered, "I don't think they do, really. It's just an excuse. Silly gudgeons."

"Gudgeons?"

"Fish, silly fish."

I wanted to smile, but said quite firmly, "William, it is not polite to call your sister and governess 'silly fish.'"

"Perhaps not—but I think they are." He bounded out of the front door and waited for me by the carriage, a mischievous smile upon his face.

The coachman, Harris, was the groom I had seen yesterday

in the stable yard. Touching his hat, he greeted me, cordially. "Good morning, m'lady. I'm to drive you to church, seeing as 'ow Trigg is with Lord Penross in Exeter."

I must have stared at him as I realized the import of his words. Then, disconcerted, I thanked him and proceeded to enter the carriage, followed by an exuberant William. So my fears had substance. Plans had not been changed, and Lord Penross had not returned last night. Then *who* was the man I had mistaken for him in the Green Room . . . ?

William was clutching my arm. "See, Aunt Charlotte— there, through the trees, you can see the church tower." He pointed out the Norman structure, and I tried to pay attention to him. The carriage started off, and in a daze I watched the trees pass by. The magnificent rhododendron bushes blazed along the driveway, but I could scarce take in their beauty. I longed to speak to someone concerning my encounter last night.

To my right I could now make out the churchyard through the trees. Then the carriage swung away, down a steep hill, and finally we passed through the wrought-iron gateway and into the village of Penross.

All was confusion in the village. The carriage came to a screeching halt, and I looked out to see a mob of people— their faces full of anger—shaking their fists at the militia who lined the high street. A wagon filled with men shackled in irons lumbered by—followed by a detachment of soldiers and what must be the King's preventive men. From inside, I tapped on the carriage roof and asked Harris what was happening.

He got down from his seat, and came to the window. "It's probably smugglers, m'lady. There's a great deal of that, what goes on 'ere." His voice sounded resigned to it, as if smuggling was a normal way of life. I had heard that Devon and Cornwall were rife with smugglers—sometimes even rendezvousing with French ships off the coast to obtain their contraband.

"Where are they taking the men?"

"Over Bodmin Moor to the assizes in Launceston. They'll be tried, and that'll be the end of that. It only needs a nod from the judge . . . he's famous for that, all right . . ."

I shuddered to think what their destiny would be.

William had been watching the scene. "Will they hang those men, Aunt Charlotte?" His face was white with concern.

"I don't know, William. But they will have to be punished in some way for breaking the law. We must remember to pray for them."

The crowds began to disperse, most following the wagon up the cobbled street and still shouting epithets. Harris cracked his whip at the horses, and we drove up to the church. As we alighted, I saw a woman sobbing in the middle of the high street, as two men restrained her from running after the wagon. I felt compelled to go and speak to her, but the coachman whispered, "Better not, m'lady. They're a rough crowd, and the mood is nasty. I've seen 'em turn on anyone who would try to 'elp."

Reluctantly, I walked with William through the lych-gate and up the winding pathway to the church. Weather-beaten gravestones lined our route, and I noted that so many bore the names of sailors and their ships. They had no doubt been killed during storms at sea—or maybe "wreckings." Smuggling. Wreckings. Cornwall had indeed a difficult and violent history. I ushered William through the doors of the ice-cold church.

The crowds had made us late, and the service had already begun. As William walked hand-in-hand with me down the aisle, I was conscious of being watched by the congregation. Their whispers mingled with the organist's prelude. We came to the Penross pew, and William stood back while I entered it. The organ stopped, but the whispering continued, until the vicar announced the opening hymn.

I hastily found the place in the hymnbook and shared it with William, who was obviously not interested in even trying to decipher the long words. I sang them from memory, whilst taking in the beauty of the old church. It was a long, low, stone building—simple in its architecture, but decorated by a magnificent gold-leaf screen that surrounded the altar. There were no flowers, it being the middle of Lent. At the end of each pew were intricate carvings of men, birds, and animals—no doubt the work of local woodcarvers.

"O God, our help in ages past, Our hope for years to come . . ." rang out through the chancel, and I felt comforted from hearing such accustomed words. For a moment,

I was no longer in an unfamiliar place of worship, but transported to the church in London, where my family had attended for so many years—Stephen, not William, standing by my side, and I, just five years old, looking up to my seven-year-old brother for my example in everything. . . .

The gleam of the highly polished brass cross on the altar caught my eye, and I prayed that Stephen—wherever he was at that moment—would be sheltered from any harm. In the pit of my stomach was a gnawing fear—and pangs of homesickness that seemed to be growing stronger each day. The events in the village had made me feel even more alien to this part of England.

We came to the end of the hymn, and the vicar's voice, asking that we be seated, interrupted my thoughts.

William tugged my sleeve as I went to make use of the foot warmer.

"Aunt Charlotte, he usually talks quite a long time," he whispered.

Putting my finger to my lips, I shook my head. William smiled up at me, settling himself against my arm.

Taking time to observe the vicar, now in the pulpit, I was pleasantly surprised. He was a distinguished man, with prematurely gray hair and fine features. Possibly in his mid-thirties, he seemed to have a warm, compelling personality. Comparisons being odious, I hastily put aside the memory of the sour-faced minister who had so devastated me at my mother's funeral. Here was a man who seemed to radiate compassion.

I began to feel less concerned with the older ladies seated near me who still kept staring quite unabashedly. Some even had moved forward in their pews to try for a closer glimpse. One of them became most bewildered when I turned to her and smiled. She immediately began to give all her attention to the vicar, and as she did so, I saw that the rest of the inquisitive women followed suit. Mother had said that a smile was worth more than gold.

The vicar's resonant voice rang out: "For my text this morning I have chosen Proverbs, chapter three, verse twenty-seven: 'Withhold not good from them to whom it is due, when it is in the power of thine hand to do it.'

"How many of us here this morning can honestly say we

have performed all the good that is within our power toward our fellowman? If we are honest, the answer would be no, we have not. Yet, we do not even have to leave this church to find people who are in great need . . ."

My thoughts of last night returned, and I wondered anew what I could do to help the unfortunate people of Penross village. I would have to speak with the vicar after the service.

William whispered, "I make toys for the children, Aunt Charlotte."

"That is most admirable, William," and I squeezed his hand—at the same time signaling with my eyes that we must be quiet and listen to the sermon.

The vicar continued, "The Lord is our example, for He never grew weary of helping those around Him—neither does He today. He works through you and me . . ."

A great warmth emanated from this man in the pulpit, and I found myself listening intently to him. Perhaps this was a man who could help me with the questions about faith that still nagged in quiet moments. The service went by so swiftly that I was amazed to hear the church bells chiming the noon hour. William and I made our way up the aisle, running the gauntlet of curious faces. I nodded to some who curtsied as I went by. Perhaps I would get to know them in the days to come.

Under the covered porch, the vicar surprised me, greeting me by name. "Lady Charlotte, it is indeed an honor to have you worship with us this morning. My name is Simon Ashford, and if I can ever be of help to you in any way, please do not hesitate to call upon me."

I thanked him and remarked how the sermon had moved me. "Perhaps we could talk later concerning it. There is much I would like to be able to do for the people in this village."

"Might I invite you for tea during the week—possibly Wednesday? My aunt, though elderly, is still famous for her delicious Cornish teas."

"It would be a pleasure, Vicar. Shall we say four o'clock?" He nodded his assent, then was interrupted by one of the inquisitive ladies, who wished to tell him what was wrong with the sermon. As I walked out with William into the crisp, blustery weather, I heard her say indignantly, "I think I've done more than my share to help these people—*and* not had a word of thanks, nor a bit of appreciation into the bargain . . ."

I caught the Reverend Mr. Simon Ashford's eye and saw a glint of amusement hovering there.

The afternoon was spent with both children. Elizabeth seemed to have retreated slightly from her hostile position and reluctantly agreed to join William and me in a walk, showing no signs of the cold that had prevented her from attending church. Several times I noticed she forgot her determination not to show me any warm feelings.

"Over there, where that group of trees is—that's what I would like to try and paint." Elizabeth's exquisite young face was animated as she ran toward the scene.

It was a beautiful dell surrounded by fir trees, and as we approached I saw that a carpet of bluebells, intermingled with primroses and daffodils, spread throughout its shady interior. Beyond and through the trees, the view of the sea was a glorious panorama. We could see for miles down the coastline—to Falmouth, toward the east, to the west, small fishing villages that seemed to creep down steep hills to the very brink of the ocean.

"Oh, yes, Elizabeth, this would be a perfect scene for us to try and put on canvas. How about tomorrow afternoon—weather permitting, of course?"

She nodded her assent, and we started to walk back toward the house. William had run on ahead, sure that he had seen a rabbit dive into a flower bed, and was busily trying to flush the animal out. Elizabeth's mood began to change as we neared the great manor. I saw a cloud of sorrow begin to fall upon her, and then came the hostility once more.

"I don't know about tomorrow, Lady Charlotte. We will have to wait and see whether it is convenient to take time to paint."

"That is perfectly all right, Elizabeth. There are many days ahead of us."

I saw her give me a quick look, as if wondering whether I was really going to stay here at Penross for any length of time.

As we entered the house, I asked her if she would come to my room for a moment—there was something I wished to give to her. She agreed, rather reluctantly, and we walked up the stairs in silence.

At the door to my room, she hesitated, and I remembered her outburst of yesterday—"This will always be my mother's room . . ." Elizabeth avoided my eyes, and I acted as if I had forgotten that anything untoward had taken place. William ran in and bounded over to the window seat, watching a ship far out on the horizon.

"Do you think it's a French ship, Aunt Charlotte, come to blow us all to pieces? Maybe Napoleon is on it!" His eyes were wide with wonder.

I laughed. "I certainly hope not, William. Please try not to let your imagination make me nervous." And yet, even though most of the French fleet had been destroyed at the battle of Trafalgar, thoughts of invasion were often crossing my mind. In London, the threat had seemed so far away.

"Now, let me find the reason I brought you here, Elizabeth." Opening the lid to my trunk, I brought out several bolts of material before I found the one I had wanted to give to her.

"Here, I want you to have this for an Easter dress." It was a yellow, sprigged muslin embroidered with small, delicate flowers. Holding it up against her, I saw that it would be perfect for her coloring.

"Oh, no, I couldn't possibly take it from you. You should have a dress made for yourself." Elizabeth obviously liked the material, but was having a battle accepting it.

"I have plenty of others to choose from," I assured her. "Where are your dresses made, Elizabeth?"

"We have always used a seamstress in the village." Elizabeth twirled before the mirror, the muslin flung over her shoulders.

"Then let us make use of her services—and soon, for Easter is only two weeks away."

Elizabeth thanked me, but I still felt a distance between us. She probably thought I was trying to buy her friendship—and in a way I was. But I also wanted her to have a new dress for Easter. I had only seen her in somber clothes which were far too old for her.

"There's enough material for a matching bonnet, Elizabeth."

She hesitated, then thanked me again. This time her eyes met mine for a second, and I could see that she was sincerely grateful.

"Don't you have a present for me, Aunt Charlotte?" William's pensive voice interrupted us.

"Well, now, surely I can find something for you." I looked through the trunk and came upon a set of lead soldiers that had belonged to Stephen. I had not wanted to part with them, yet I knew William would enjoy the brilliantly painted toys.

"If you promise to take great care of these soldiers, you may have them, William. They were my brother, Stephen's. Remember, I told you he is with the Coldstream Guards, fighting Napoleon?"

"Oh, yes, I remember. Thank you, Aunt Charlotte; I will take great care of them." He ran to the window seat and began lining them up. "They will guard Penross against Napoleon, you'll see."

It had been a pleasant afternoon, and I was sorry when the children had to leave for their supper. Miss Marsden was most disapproving of the material I had given Elizabeth. However, I did not let this dissuade me in any way, and I told the governess I would be sending for the seamstress the next day.

William had left a line of the toy soldiers on the window seat. "To guard you during the night, Aunt Charlotte," he had said, very seriously. I smiled, remembering his concern.

After another lonely, depressing meal in the great dining hall, I decided to go to the music room and play the pianoforte. Music had always had a way of helping me forget my loneliness, and I poured out my emotions in the compositions of Mozart that now filled the vast room. A bridge of understanding between composer and player seemed to give me solace.

I played several marches and mazurkas and was in the midst of an aria from "The Magic Flute" when I sensed someone had come into the room. The light from the candelabrum on the pianoforte obstructed my view, yet I was conscious of another's presence.

A cold sweat was upon my brow, and I found it difficult to concentrate upon my playing. Finally I came to the last note, and sat—rigid—not daring to move.

"Superb! Your Mozart is as brilliant as your Haydn and Bach. Bravo!"

I spun round on the music bench upon hearing the familiar voice. Lord Penross was standing in the shadows—a broad smile upon his face.

Seeing my fright, he apologized. "I did not mean to startle you, Lady Charlotte, but I refrained from interrupting such inspired playing."

I rose to my feet and walked over to welcome him.

"We were not expecting you until tomorrow, Lord Penross."

He did not respond. And I searched his eyes, hoping that an answer from him would give some indication as to whether he had really gone away, or whether it was he—after all—whom I had encountered in the Green Room last night. But he merely asked if I would join him in the library for some hot chocolate and give him news concerning his children, and in the candlelight his dark eyes were unreadable. He turned, and I followed him from the room.

8

*L*ow, gray clouds foretold that a violent storm would soon be breaking. The view from the breakfast room was fast becoming obliterated by a dense mist rolling in from the sea. Plans for riding with William this morning would have to be canceled. How I dreaded a day cooped up in this oppressive house. My feelings of uneasiness could be assuaged by being free to ride over the gorse-covered moors with my powerful horse beneath me. Guardian was a noble animal, from fine stock, sensitive to the least direction I gave him. I was grateful to Lord Penross for his generosity in giving me access to such a creature.

"You are deep in thought this morning, Lady Charlotte." Lord Penross's voice startled me, for I had been miles away. "Pardon me, I was thinking that it looked as if we were in for a stormy day. I had hoped to ride this morning with William."

"There will soon be good weather. These storms come and go here—it's a part of our lives. The southwesterly wind is the culprit . . ." He folded the *Times* and put it down by his plate, giving me his full attention.

I could not deny the fact that I found him most attractive. His eyes searched mine, and I had to turn and look out at the mist once more. His moods were like the storms in Cornwall—angry, sometimes destructive, but quickly passing. And once they were gone, he seemed unaware that they had caused any havoc whatsoever. I looked back at him, and he smiled as if knowing my thoughts.

I remembered Elizabeth's outburst upon seeing her mother's book in my room, and I wondered whether I should tell him about the incident. He would see that the book had been returned to the library. It would be best if I apprised him of the situation. So I gently described the scene and said I felt it best that we consider her feelings—she was still so deeply sensitive concerning her mother.

"Very well, if you think I should not discuss it with her. I trust she was not rude to you." He looked directly at me. "The children have accepted you, have they not?"

"William has completely, it would seem. With Elizabeth it will take a little more time. I understand her feelings."

Lord Penross rose and went back to the sideboard for a second helping. "And how do you get on with Miss Marsden?" His voice was pointed, and he was obviously waiting for a full report.

"That relationship also needs time, Lord Penross." I longed to ask him why he had ever allowed her to be his children's governess, but I refrained. "She seems to be a very capable teacher. The children are well advanced . . ."

"Good—then it seems as if everything is under control." He walked back to the table, his plate laden once more with a selection from each of the silver-covered dishes. Seated, he informed me, "I shall not be here for luncheon—my agent has told me that there are many problems at the mines, and I am needed to try to quell a possible rebellion amongst the men."

"I am indeed sorry to hear that. I trust you will find the situation less volatile than is anticipated."

As Lord Penross had stood at the sideboard, with his back toward me, I had tried clearly to remember the silhouette of the man in the Green Room. It had looked so like him. Yet, *had* there been a different tilt to his head—had the shoulders been less broad . . . ?

I summoned up the courage to ask him if it were he whom I had encountered the other night. "Lord Penross . . ." He looked up quickly from the *Times,* a look of slight irritation upon his brow. My courage failed, and I asked lamely, "Was your trip to Exeter a satisfactory one?"

"Somewhat. I always detest the long coach ride . . ." His attention went back to the newspaper once more, and I wondered if he were trying to evade my question.

There was a knock upon the door and Rogers entered, looking rather disturbed.

"Lord Penross, there are three men from the constabulary asking if they might have a word with you." Rogers stopped as Lord Penross turned to him. "I believe it's about the smuggling that went on last Saturday night, m'lord."

There was an uneasy silence between the two men, then Lord Penross said hastily, "Well, show them in, Rogers—don't just stand there."

I saw Rogers's face take on a resentful expression, and he glanced over at me—angry, possibly, that Lord Penross had been curt to him in my presence.

"I know nothing of this. Had you heard of any smuggling, Lady Charlotte?" Lord Penross seemed almost resigned to the news—the local men, apparently, were often being arrested for such a crime.

"On my way to church yesterday, I saw the King's preventive men taking about seven or eight prisoners to Launceston. The coachman informed me of their possible fate. It was most distressing to William and myself . . ."

Another knock upon the door, and Rogers ushered in three burly men, each of them bowing upon seeing Lord Penross and being introduced to me. The eldest one, who must be the head constable, was most apologetic at seeing that he had interrupted our breakfast.

"Beggin' yer pardon, m'lord. I regret 'aving to call at such an early 'our, but needs be we 'ave evidence we would like to share with ye, and perhaps ask a few questions."

I rose to leave, feeling that this interview should not include me, and excused myself to Lord Penross, who handed me the *Times* with a quick smile. On reaching the door, I hesitated for a moment, then looked back at the constables.

My voice trembled as I asked, "Do you know the fate of the men who were taken from the village yesterday to Launceston assizes?"

The chief constable replied flatly, "They were to be 'anged this morning—at daybreak, m'lady."

I hastily left the room and stood for a moment in the hall, trying to compose myself. The memory of the woman left crying in the high street brought tears to my own eyes, and I ran up the stairs, avoiding Mrs. Dawson, who had been trying to find out what was going on in the breakfast room.

Those men had committed a crime. But, dear God, hanging was far too severe a punishment. Their families would greatly suffer—not only now, from their bereavement, but for years to come, for they had lost their providers.

I closed the door to my room and went over to the window, looking out toward the stormy, restless sea. The mist had almost covered it from view. I prayed for all those who would be affected by the men's deaths, asking the Lord to comfort their hearts that day.

Getting up from my knees, I walked back toward the door, remembering that I must tell William we would have to wait until tomorrow for our ride. The view from the west window seemed even more menacing as the mist curled around the sharp, jagged rocks. I remembered the men I had seen at Tregoran Cove, and I wondered if they had had any part in last Saturday night's smuggling.

Then I recalled the low, heavy rumbling I had heard outside my window that same night. Could I have heard wagons laden with smugglers' spoils? I trembled at the thought that there might be people involved here at Penross Manor . . .

Should I tell the constable of the strange noises? In no way did I want to involve Lord Penross in any of this, yet was it not my duty to give any information I had concerning the matter?

And Lord Penross himself—had he really stayed here and not gone to Exeter . . . ?

A light tap at the door made me collect my thoughts. I hastily found a handkerchief and wiped my eyes, telling whoever it was to come in.

It was William, complete with riding crop in hand.

"You're not ready, Aunt Charlotte." Disappointment was written on his face.

"We'll have to postpone our ride today, William. The weather is about to break, and we don't want to get caught in a storm." I replaced my handkerchief in the cuff of my sleeve.

"You've been crying, haven't you, Aunt Charlotte?" He came over and put his hand in mine.

I looked down at William, not wanting to let him know the reason for my tears. He had been so concerned about the men in the wagon yesterday.

William smiled up at me. "Don't worry—we'll be able to ride tomorrow, I'm sure." He looked over to the window seat, where he had left Stephen's toy soldiers.

"And look—they're still guarding you from Napoleon. Don't be afraid, Aunt Charlotte."

I hugged him to me—this dear, loving child. "I won't be—not with you and those soldiers to take care of me."

A splatter of rain hit the window and trickled down the pane; the impending storm had begun. I hoped with all my heart that it did not foretell the beginning of an even greater storm within the walls of Penross.

9

*T*he violent storm continued all morning, and deafening thunder often interrupted the Latin lesson I had begun with the children. Miss Marsden was feeling unwell, so I took advantage of the extra hours. However, William thought it was a waste of time to learn even one word of a dead language. Elizabeth proved to be a valiant defender.

"William, this seemingly 'useless' language is where we derived our own, so hush—and pay attention."

I watched, amused, as the two fell into a fierce argument on the subject.

Finally, under great duress, William began to learn his first Latin words—"Porto, portas, portat . . . ugh! Latin is *so* boring . . ."

His venture into the world of music proved to be a much happier one. He chose to learn the flute, and he spent an amusing half hour trying to coax sounds out of the instrument I had brought, while Elizabeth practiced scales upon the pianoforte. There was an instant rapport to the world of music, and I could sense delightful days ahead as they explored this new adventure.

"We shall have to learn something soon, Elizabeth, so that we can play a duet for Papa!"

William's reference to his father reminded me that Lord Penross would not be home for lunch, and I had not heard the result of the constable's visit with him. The news of the smuggling had cast an even greater pall upon the vast house, and I was greatly concerned. Glancing out of the lofty windows of the music room, I wondered how Lord Penross was faring at the mines. The streams of water pouring down the glass almost obliterated any view of the outside. The rain would do nothing to dampen the frenzied anger of the miners; I hoped that Lord Penross would be safe. More and more, I was finding that he invaded my thoughts . . .

But for now, the inclement weather forgotten, and the troubled news of this morning unknown to the children, the music room was filled with their first foray into a hitherto unknown accomplishment. With such a magnificent pianoforte, I was surprised that at least Elizabeth had never learned before. I wanted to ask whether their mother had ever played, but resisted the thought. The memory of Elizabeth's resentment toward me was still too fresh to risk my intruding into her memories.

After lunch, the weather cleared, and it was not long before I was informed that the seamstress had arrived to fit Elizabeth for her Easter dress.

I went with Elizabeth to my room—the bright, sheer material was still draped upon the chaise lounge. Elizabeth wore an air of suppressed excitement while she waited for the seamstress.

My back was toward the door when the woman entered. I had remembered that in my trunk was some yellow ribbon which would perfectly match the material, and I was in the midst of finding it. After a few seconds, I turned around to greet the seamstress, and as I did my mouth fell open in surprise.

She was the woman I had seen crying in the street the day before—the one who had been restrained from running after the wagon filled with the shackled men. Her eyes were still red-rimmed, and the shadows beneath them bore evidence of her ordeal.

Upon recovering from my shock, I welcomed the woman. Elizabeth immediately ran to the material, explaining exactly how she would like her new dress to look.

I found it difficult to concentrate. My feelings for the seamstress and my awareness of the men's fate caused me to forget the reason the woman had come to Penross. Standing there, oblivious to the bright yellow ribbon in my hand, I could not help but wonder if she knew of the sentence that had possibly been carried out this very morning.

"I'm Mrs. Johns, m'lady." Bobbing a curtsy, she continued, rather breathlessly, "I would have been 'ere sooner, but what with the weather, me children . . . and other . . . circumstances . . ." I saw that tears were not far off, and I went over to her.

"Please do not apologize, Mrs. Johns. I quite understand." I wanted to tell her that I had seen the tragic "circumstances" in the high street and had wished to speak with her there, but now Elizabeth's presence stopped me. So I listened with a heavy heart as the seamstress attempted to behave as if her life had not been shattered by the events of Saturday night— "My, you've grown, Miss Elizabeth, since last I was 'ere."

I watched her intently. She appeared to be in her late thirties, and was dressed in what was probably her "Sunday best"—more than likely a castoff from one of her customers. The material, a faded, deep-rose silk, was far too luxurious for her to afford new. Her hands looked as if they belonged to a much older woman—hard work had indeed left its mark. The lusterless brown hair, caught back in a straggly knot, framed a sad, gaunt face.

Elizabeth found it difficult to stand still while Mrs. Johns proceeded to measure her for the new dress. I had not seen the child so excited, and I was glad I had thought of the idea. She needed a bright distraction in her relatively dull life. Mrs. Johns finished measuring, and I gave instructions for completing the new dress and asked if she would make a bonnet from the remaining material. It was only then that I realized I had been crushing the yellow ribbon in my hands.

With assurances that a "good 'ot iron will take them creases out, m'lady," and that the dress would be ready for Easter, Mrs. Johns departed.

Elizabeth waited behind in my room and turned to thank me. "It was a pleasure, Elizabeth. You are going to look lovely in it."

At that moment, Miss Marsden knocked on my door and broke the happy mood between us. "I think that Elizabeth has wasted far too much of her school time already, Lady

Charlotte. There are more important ways for her to spend this afternoon."

Elizabeth's whole mood changed. With an almost guilty look, she hurriedly followed Miss Marsden, not even looking back toward me. Miss Marsden certainly had the gift of being able to destroy any happy moments for the child. The finished dress would no doubt be met with the same icy disapproval . . .

I returned to thinking about Mrs. Johns, and wondered what I could do to help this woman. The meager earnings of a seamstress in Penross village would not be sufficient for her to feed her family adequately. I thought again of the dress she had been wearing. It had seemed so incongruous on her—the faded silk and carefully mended lace trim looking so out of place against the rough, worn hands. Poor woman—who had given it to her? I would have to ask the vicar what could be done to help this family . . .

Thoughts of the vicar made me realize the time. It was almost a quarter to four, and I was due at the vicarage on the hour. I rang the bell-pull and asked Ellie to see that my horse was brought to the front door. It would be pleasant to ride down to the church; I would take the shortcut through the woods . . .

Guardian proved to be most dexterous, and he weaved his way through the trees—I had to bend low to avoid having the branches snatch at my plumed riding hat. The air was crisp and fresh after the storm, but leaden clouds still remained overhead. The muddied paths often proved to be quite treacherous. Guardian slipped several times, but righted himself with a protesting neigh, and trotted onward.

We reached the churchyard, and I saw that the quickest way to the vicarage was a pathway that wound around some ancient gravestones. It was an eerie part of the graveyard, although the path did prove faster than the more conventional one. Dark, overhanging vines, growing in thick profusion, brushed my face, and raindrops fell from the disturbed branches as I rode by. I was more than thankful when I reached the end of the path and saw the vicarage before me.

Alighting, I tied Guardian to one of the large metal rings

in the wall. I remembered the night I had passed by the churchyard in Lord Penross's coach and had seen a light in one of the vicarage windows. A hasty impression of a man reading a large book, sitting by the fire, came back to me, and I realized that it must have been the Reverend Mr. Simon Ashford, with whom I was now to have tea.

I rang the rusted bell-pull and, while waiting for the door to open, brushed the raindrops off my riding habit and took the opportunity to look around me. The dark stone house was in need of repair. The shutters hung at odd angles, their hinges desperately needing the attention of a carpenter. The small garden was hopelessly overgrown, although brightly colored spring flowers were valiantly pushing their way upward through a mass of tangled, constricting weeds. Looking across the street at the whitewashed cottages, with their snug thatched roofs and small, walled gardens, I noticed that each one had a mass of flowers growing within the confines of its garden.

The vicarage door swung open, and I turned to find the Reverend Mr. Ashford standing there.

"Lady Charlotte, how delighted I am to see you. Please come into my humble abode. You will see that a bachelor lives here, I fear. . . . My dear aunt is quite elderly and unable to keep up with everything. However, she is delighted you accepted my invitation—she is always happy to provide tea."

I stepped over the threshold into a dark, dismal hallway. The hatstand was crowded with odd coats, scarves, and hats, plus a bouquet of umbrellas—each looking as if the Cornish gales had wreaked utter destruction upon it.

The vicar ushered me into a cluttered living room piled high with books and papers and filled with a strange selection of furniture. I now saw the fireplace and chair close by. "This is not the first time, Vicar, I have seen your living room" and I told him of the night of my arrival.

"What a storm to have greeted you, Lady Charlotte. Cornwall has many beautiful days. I trust you will soon be enjoying them." He pointed to an upright, upholstered chair. "Here, I think you will find this the most comfortable of the odd assortment I seem to have been left with. I 'inherited' this collection upon taking up the living at St. Michael's Church!"

Mr. Ashford smiled, walked over to the fireplace, and proceeded to stir the coals. "When one decides to go into the Church, objects like elegant furniture take a decided back seat, shall we say?" His eyes twinkled, and I found myself thinking again that he was indeed a most pleasant and warm representative of his calling.

The living room door swung open, and in came a smiling, rather rotund woman in her late sixties. Silvery gray hair peeked out from her white mob cap, and a pair of steel spectacles balanced precariously at the end of her nose. She carried a large tray, upon which were all the necessities for an enormous, waist-expanding tea—Cornish cream; strawberry jam; large, homemade scones; fruitcake; saffron cakes; and more.

The vicar introduced her to me—"Mrs. Wills, my aunt—famous for her Cornish teas."

She curtsied, leaving the groaning tray on a small table, and then walked back toward the door. "I trust you will find it all to your liking, m'lady."

I assured her that the tea looked delicious, at the same time wondering how I would ever begin to make even a small-sized dent in such a vast spread. But my fears were soon allayed when I saw the large portions to which Mr. Ashford helped himself. The enormous mounds of Cornish cream and homemade jam that found their way on to his plate were quite remarkable.

As I was about to take my first sip of tea, the vicar remarked apologetically, "I trust you will not find the tea too unpleasant, Lady Charlotte. With it now costing seven shillings a pound, my aunt has to resort to making it from burnt cake and wholemeal bread . . ."

After tasting it, I decided to drink the rest as slowly as was possible.

During our conversation, I noticed a finely embroidered sampler with words by the Reverend John Wesley, the Methodist preacher, that were reminiscent of Mr. Ashford's Sunday sermon.

> Do all the good you can
> In all the ways you can,
> In all the places you can,

71

At all the times you can,
To all the people you can,
As long as ever you can.

A small Staffordshire figure of John Wesley was prominently displayed upon the mantlepiece. Both it and the sampler seemed out of place in a Church of England vicarage. I asked, "Is it not unusual to see the reverend gentleman represented within the vicarage of the established Church?"

The Reverend Mr. Ashford smiled. "Indeed, it is. But, he had such an influence on my life when I was a very young boy. It was he who was really instrumental in my deciding to take the Church as my calling. I heard him preach over at Gwennap when he was eighty years of age, and as I listened it seemed that God was speaking to me. Wesley moved my heart in a way that it had never been moved before."

"What did he say that made such a difference?"

"He told of our Lord's love and concern for each one of us, and said that we all needed to know Him in a real, living way. He made it all so personal. He made me see it is not enough to say by rote the printed service in our prayer books—it must come from our hearts."

"Then why did you become a minister in the Church of England?"

"My father would not hear of my joining any Nonconformist group, and I felt that I could be used by God within the texture of this Church. I feel I made the right decision. Gradually, the Church of England is beginning to accept those with differing views as being part of the true Church, also."

Offering me a saffron cake, he continued, "Actually, it was never Wesley's intention that his followers should leave the Church. Even when he lay dying, he pleaded that there be no dissension."

I said nothing, but this warm, gentle man had touched on a sensitive nerve within me. I had many questions to be answered concerning my faith. Perhaps later I would be able to open up my heart to him and he could help me find the answers to many of my questions. Already, through his influence, I was feeling stronger in my faith.

The seamstress, Mrs. Johns, was brought into our

conversation, and I learned she had to care for three children, all under ten years of age. The Reverend Ashford had not heard of any executions at Launceston. "I trust that the constable's surmise was incorrect, Lady Charlotte. I have personally sent word to the judge at the assizes, asking for leniency. Many of these men are desperate to help their families, for the twenty years of war with France have drained so much from this area."

"But surely the mines, the farms, the fishing are all needed and bring good revenue?"

Mr. Ashford hesitated before going on, and only then did he speak with reluctance. "I'm afraid the men are dissatisfied with their earnings from the Penross estate. It would seem that Lord Penross has not kept up with the times. Rather, the feudal system has become more and more restrictive." Stirring his tea thoughtfully, he continued, "All England is feeling the ferment of revolution—you probably know that already there have been riots in the North. I would not be surprised to see something violent happen— akin to what occurred in France."

"You mean, the aristocracy here could be treated like those in Paris. Surely, the people of England would not be that bloodthirsty?" I shuddered to think that Madame Guillotine's equivalent could be experienced here.

But that was not the problem at hand. "What can we do to help these people? I have only a small allowance from my inheritance, but living at Penross I will now have but minor expenses. I would like to be able to give you some money for Mrs. Johns and her family, and for others who are in great need. It is a far cry from what is required, but at least it might be a start. I will talk with Lord Penross this evening and perhaps muster his support."

"It is indeed generous of you, Lady Charlotte, and I would gladly accept any small contributions. But you must not expect Lord Penross to respond to your appeal. He has been having great difficulty himself trying to keep up the estate, and I have found him to be unapproachable concerning these matters." The vicar drew a long sigh and sat forward, looking into the fire. "I believe what is needed is our prayers . . . for God alone can perform the miracle required."

"You have the assurance of my prayers, Mr. Ashford. If

73

there is any other way I can be of help to the people of this village, please let me know." Tea now over, I rose to leave, and gathering up my gloves and riding crop, started to walk toward the door.

"There *is* something else you can do, Lady Charlotte. The small prison here needs a lady to visit occasionally. There are women who have been incarcerated, some for many months, and who have no visitors."

The thought of visiting such a dismal place did not appeal to me, yet I could not refuse. "Of course, Vicar, I will ask Lord Penross what days would be convenient to leave the children."

I looked over to the mantle clock and saw that tea would have been over some time ago at Penross. I had promised to read to William.

Mr. Ashford escorted me out of the vicarage and watched as I untethered Guardian. The great, rusty ring made it difficult for me to untie his rein, and the vicar offered to help me.

"Allow me . . . I'm used to this, Lady Charlotte." His strong fingers soon had the horse freed. "Did you notice the rings on the columns in the church on Sunday?"

I had noticed them, for they had left great rust marks, and I had wondered why a church would have needed them there in the first place.

"During the Civil War, St. Michael's was turned into a stable for Cromwell's cavalry. The christening font became a watering trough. Of course, the building has changed considerably since then. . . . Incidentally, Penross Manor featured greatly in the war—many Royalists were hidden within its walls."

"I saw a framed letter from Charles II in the chapel. It thanked the Lord Penross of the day for all his help . . ."

"Ah, yes, I have seen it, too. I hear there are several priests' holes within Penross. They were secret hiding places used in Queen Elizabeth's reign—when priests were hunted and persecuted for celebrating the forbidden Mass. There is one, I believe, in the eastern turret."

I turned to look at him. "Are you sure?" My heart began beating faster.

"Why yes. I'm surprised that Lord Penross has not told you about the idiosyncrasies of his manor."

Mounting my horse, I thought of the man whom I had seen in the Green Room—and of the door in the paneling. Could it be that someone was in hiding? I hesitated for a moment, then drew courage to ask Mr. Ashford a question for which, thus far, I had been unable to find an answer.

"Vicar, how did Lady Penross die?"

There was a long pause. Deep in thought, the vicar looked away from me. "If you haven't been told, perhaps it's not my place to say, Lady Charlotte."

"I shall tell no one where I obtained my information."

Guardian was by now anxious to leave, and I had to rein him in quite sharply.

Reluctantly, the Reverend Simon Ashford looked up at me and said soberly, "Very well, Lady Charlotte. She was murdered. Lord Penross found her in the Green Room. From then on, the east wing has never been used . . ."

10

In the quickly fading light, I decided to return to Penross by way of the main driveway, and rode Guardian through the gates as fast as was possible. The thought of returning to London was becoming more and more urgent to me. I dreaded to think of having to live under the roof of Penross Manor for any length of time—even more so now that the vicar had told me of Lady Penross's tragic death.

But the prospect of traveling to London with Trigg was unbearable to me. I would write my aunt, Lady Sanford, and ask her to send a coach for me.

But then . . . thoughts of the children made me reconsider—for they were growing more dear to me each day. I could not abandon them to the restrictive, gloomy Miss Marsden.

And Lord Penross—I felt myself more and more drawn to him. Yet now there was also this overwhelming suspicion that perhaps it was he who had been responsible for his wife's murder . . .

The driveway twisted and turned, and the dense woods on either side became more and more frightening to me, for there was now barely any light. I urged Guardian on until we rounded a corner, and there before me was the resplendent yet frightening Penross Manor. Reining in the horse, I sat for a moment looking up at the great house, and my eyes once again were drawn immediately to the eastern turret.

There were no lights burning from its small, diamond-paned windows. Yet, I still had that ominous sensation that someone was watching me.

The main house already gleamed with candlelight, which cast elongated images of the windows across the flower beds and spilled onto the driveway and lawns. A sudden impulse directed me to ride toward the eastern turret. If there were a priest hole within its walls, then perhaps there might be a secret entrance to the house. I dismounted, and with the pretense of picking the violets that grew in profusion at the turret's base, I worked my way to where it met the main wall of the house.

At first, I saw nothing. Then, as I walked around to the northern side, I observed a gap between the tower wall and the main house. Edging my way toward it, I could see that there was enough room for someone to push his way through. The ground was muddy from the recent storm, but I was determined to find out where the opening led. I pushed my way into it, and discovered a small anteroom. It was completely dark, save for a glimmer of light shining from one of the windows in the main house, and I could just make out the latch on a narrow door. Lifting it, I found the door swung open easily, revealing a flight of stone steps leading up into the tower. On the first step was a bundle of candles and a tinderbox.

The sound of footsteps in the driveway outside caused me to shut the door and edge my way out of the turret. I continued to pick more of the small flowers, and saw that one of the gardeners was walking toward me. He raised his hat, while looking down at the bunch of violets in my hand.

" 'Tis too muddy for ye to be picking flowers, m'lady. I could've done that for ye . . ." He spoke kindly, yet I saw a look of annoyance—and distrust.

"Oh, I noticed them as I was riding by and thought how much they would brighten my room. Strange that the violet, such a delicate flower, would have been chosen as Napoleon's emblem, is it not?" The gardener snorted his disapproval as I walked ahead of him—at the same time trying to scrape some of the mud from my riding boots. "You maintain a spectacular garden—you must feel proud of your work."

"Oh, yes, m'lady . . . that I am."

He stood there, still watching me, as I led Guardian to the main door of the house and tied him to a post.

Running up the steps, I was greeted by Rogers.

"Lord Penross is waiting for you in the drawing room, m'lady." His face bore a rather satisfied look—which seemed to prophesy a troubled meeting with Lord Penross. I asked Rogers to see that the groom took Guardian back to the stables and, removing my gloves, left them and my riding crop in the hall.

As I approached the drawing room, the door was open and I saw Lord Penross standing by the fireplace. His back was toward me, his hands resting on the mantlepiece, and as I entered he angrily kicked one of the logs. I saw that he was in a most belligerent mood.

Upon hearing the rustle of my skirt, he swung around and stood looking at me. The anger in his eyes did not prevent a momentary look of admiration: "Well, Lady Charlotte, you do indeed cut a fine figure in your riding habit." His eyes swept from my plumed hat, all the way down to my muddied riding boots.

"Thank you, Lord Penross."

We stood looking at one another for a few moments. I did not know whether to walk toward him and sit down, to ask him how his day had been, or merely to await what promised to be an inquisition concerning my whereabouts. It started soon enough.

"I see you are a nature lover. Tell me, does it take several hours to pick such a puny bunch of flowers?"

I looked down at the violets in my hand. "No, only a few moments."

There was an explosive glint in his eyes, and I could tell that he already knew where I had been for the last two hours. It baffled me, though, that he should object quite so vehemently.

"I am sure that one of the servants must have told you that I took tea with the vicar." My chin was raised as I stood my ground.

"Lady Charlotte, I was unaware that when I asked that you come to Penross to be a companion for my children it would involve socializing with the local clergy. William has been down here several times asking for you. You apparently promised that you would read to him . . ."

"I did promise, Lord Penross, and was on my way when Rogers said you wished to speak with me."

"A trifle late," he said scathingly.

"Then if you have no more to say to me, I will go to him immediately." I abruptly turned to leave, but Lord Penross called me back.

"I would like to ask what conversation you had with the vicar. What was so pressing that you had to see him?"

"Perhaps you are weary and not in the mood to hear at this time, Lord Penross. It must have been a hard day for you at the mines."

"Indeed it was, and I did not expect to come home to a household thrown into disarray by your personal excursions. Miss Marsden informs me that you are already disrupting the children's schedule."

So the dour governess had already begun to make trouble for me. I was not surprised.

"If bringing some joy into their lives is a disruption, then I plead guilty. The children and I have had a most pleasant day. William learned his first Latin, and he and Elizabeth are hoping to surprise you soon with a duet on the flute and pianoforte."

"You say nothing of seamstresses—or brightly colored material from London—completely unsuitable for my daughter."

"I would ask that you be the judge of that when you see her in her Easter dress. A young girl should surely be allowed to wear bright colors, Lord Penross." My anger was mounting.

"Very well, I will make my judgment upon seeing the finished garment." He walked back toward the fireplace, and looked down into the fire, returning to an earlier subject. "Tell me, what did you discuss at the vicarage?"

"I merely wanted to know, after hearing the vicar's sermon on Sunday—when he asked the congregation if we were doing everything in our power to help our fellowman—what I could personally do. I had wondered if part of my allowance could go to help the poor in the village.

And I had hoped perhaps I could enlist your support, also."

Lord Penross exploded. "Am I not doing enough by offering you a home and a living? Do you also have to offer money which I can ill afford at this time to be squandered?"

"Squandered? To help some poor soul whose husband has been killed—either by the hangman or by Napoleon's army—do you call that squandering?" My voice was now raised, and I regretted almost losing control.

My words went deep with Lord Penross, and I saw him begin to change his mood. "Yes," he said quietly, "there are many who are suffering at this time. I only wish I could help—but you don't seem to realize that I have also been affected by the war. The Penross family fortune is fast disappearing—just as yours has."

His arms stretched out in a hopeless gesture as he continued, "Apart from the war, the mines are beginning to run dry of their resources of tin, and unless new shafts produce satisfactory lodes, I shall have to close them." Wearily, he added, "This is what I have been trying to tell the miners today."

"I am sorry, Lord Penross. I did not wish to add to your burdens. But I do believe that if we all work together, with God, then some of these problems can be eradicated."

Lord Penross gave a short laugh. "You do sound as if you have just had tea with the vicar! It will take more than a few prayers to solve the problems of Penross."

Secretly, I felt he might be right, but I would not concede the point to him. Instead, I answered politely, "I remember, when I first came here, that you asked me to make your children cognizant of the teachings of the Church. I believe one of the main beliefs is that God does hear and answer our prayers."

There was a hint of a smile as Lord Penross whispered, "Touché, Lady Charlotte. Do not judge me by today—it has been one of the worst I have encountered."

I thought that surely the worst must have been the day he found his wife murdered . . .

"Was there anything else you discussed with the vicar?" I felt Lord Penross's questioning look bore right through me.

"We talked of the history of Penross—of the time of Charles II—how many Royalists were hidden within these walls . . ."

Lord Penross had a faraway look . . . "Ah, yes. The vicar is a great historian. That was all?"

I was hesitating, unwilling to tell him that I now knew of Lady Penross's murder, when William came running in.

"You are supposed to knock before entering a room," Lord Penross bellowed.

"Sorry, Papa, but I heard that Aunt Charlotte had returned." He ran to me and took my hand. "Miss Marsden says you won't be able to read to me if we don't start soon."

"If your Father will excuse me, then we can go up and start immediately." I turned to look at Lord Penross.

"By all means. Your Aunt Charlotte and I have finished our conversation—for now. We can continue it during dinner . . ."

I put my arm around William's shoulder, and we left the room. There was a magnetic sensation that ran down my spine, and I looked back to see Lord Penross staring at me—a mysterious expression in his eyes.

Why was he so concerned regarding my conversation with the vicar? Did he suspect that I now knew the Green Room's terrible secret . . . ?

11

We partook of a stilted dinner that night—embarrassing for the lack of conversation. Lord Penross remained suspicious of my visit with the vicar, and his attitude did nothing to allay my feelings of concern regarding the death of his wife. Also, if someone were in hiding, was he aware of it? His complex nature made me wary of asking any questions. I feared what his response might be.

Several times during the next two weeks, I started to write to my aunt, asking her to send down her coach from London for me. Yet, in spite of my growing fears I felt compelled to remain—at least for a while. William had asked me whether I would really be staying on at Penross—"I'm so much happier with you here, Aunt Charlotte."

Elizabeth remained slightly aloof and gave little indication that she was glad I had come to live at Penross. Several times she tried to be friendly, but as soon as Miss Marsden appeared on the scene, she retreated into her shell of indifference.

Each time I encountered Miss Marsden, I felt the same icy tension that had greeted me at our first meeting. I would see her studying me from afar, and she seemed to have a close relationship with Mrs. Dawson—who obviously resented me, too.

"Lady Penross would not have allowed this . . ." was Mrs. Dawson's frequent retort when I ordered some treat for the children or suggested a change in the menu. I could see that I had to tread my way carefully so as not to disrupt a household that was run to the letter each waking moment.

My days began to take on a decided pattern, and with Lord Penross's permission I found that I was able to help—if only in a small way—with the needs of the villagers. Clothes that had been stored in many of the vast attics were sorted and given to the church for distribution in the parish. I visited the small prison in the village and was horrified by the smell, the crowding, the disease. There were arguments with Lord Penross concerning whether it was proper for me to be seen in such a place, but I stood my ground and suggested that he speak with the local constabulary concerning the deplorable state in which I had found the women. There were promises that conditions would become more humane, but they were slow in coming, and I had to continue to badger the authorities.

News of the hanging of the men I had seen in the wagon had been confirmed. Shaken, I visited Mrs. Johns in her small, sparsely furnished cottage and offered my sympathy. She looked gaunt—her eyes haunted, but her mien was most courageous. The children were thin and obviously in need of nourishing food. I tried in any way I could to help alleviate their suffering, but nothing could replace the man who had, tragically, been lured by the "smugglers' moon."

Lord Penross was often away, and I spent many evenings playing the pianoforte, writing letters—mostly to Stephen and my aunt—or reading in the vast library. It was always the evenings that I dreaded, for the days were filled with either teaching the children, visiting in the village, riding with William, or venturing over the moors on my own with Guardian.

I had become increasingly aware of the "ha-ha" ditches that surrounded the park of Penross (the ones about which Lord Penross had warned William) and several times had almost come unseated. However, Guardian seemed to have a sixth sense concerning them and most of the time would jump effortlessly over their wide expanses.

The view from the top of the moors, directly behind the great manor house, was everchanging—for the skies with their different moods cast an almost magical cover of color. Sometimes the gorse-covered hills shone with the brilliance of gold. Other times, when the leaden skies foretold an imminent storm, the whole countryside took on a gray, frightening countenance, and the wind roared through weirdly contorted trees. Cormorants and sea gulls screamed their protest and swooped overhead, defying the elements.

Far in the distance rose the chimneys of the mines: their starkness incongruous against the wild, rugged countryside. No smoke bellowed from their blackened stacks, and the days grew more tense as the continued search for a new lode of tin appeared to be in vain. I wondered how long Lord Penross could put off closing the mines, and thus plunging many families into complete poverty.

Looking at Penross from the height of the moors, I would often imagine what it must have been like in its heyday, when there was money enough to make use of all the wings of the house. Now, the Penrosses were reduced to living in only the main west wing, which might also have to be given up eventually.

The chapel always drew my attention—the thought of the beautiful Lady Penross buried within its walls continually revived unanswered questions . . .

Upon the second anniversary of Lady Penross's death, I paid special attention to the children. Elizabeth chose to be on her own, spending many hours in her room—but William clung to my hand often during the day, as if afraid that I, too, would leave him. When Elizabeth did join us, I could see she had been crying. In the afternoon, the two children asked if they could go and pick some flowers to take to the chapel, and I watched them from my window. Tears coursed down my cheeks as I thought about the crime that had so cruelly deprived them of their mother . . .

It was several days later, while taking a walk, that I decided to visit the chapel once more. It seemed even darker than before, for the skies were overcast, and there was no flood of colored light from the windows. I walked down toward the altar and saw that the children's flowers, in a small vase, were accompanied by a bunch of roses, which had been merely placed on the ground near Lady Penross's memorial. Lord Penross had been away for over a week, so I knew that they could not have been left by him.

It was while I was looking down at the flowers that I had a most terrifying feeling sweep over me. I felt that I was not alone in the chapel—that someone was near me. At that moment all I knew was that I had to get out into the daylight, and I turned and ran up the aisle. For a few seconds the latch on the door stuck, and I almost panicked, but eventually I was able to unlock the door and run into the courtyard. I did not believe it was my imagination. Someone was in the chapel, and whoever was there did not bode me well . . .

There was an ever-constant watch toward the sea, for Napoleon had managed to reassemble his Grande Armee and was threatening to turn Europe into chaos once more. Stephen's letters were becoming less and less frequent, and I would not have been surprised to hear that he and his regiment had departed for overseas.

One stormy, violent night, a French brigantine collided with one of our ships, and all hands were lost. For days, the coastline was strewn with wreckage, and the miners and fishermen had managed to outwit the King's preventive men by collecting many of the spoils during the dead of night. Once more, Lord Penross forbade any of us to go near the sea—for fighting over the loot was vicious and completely out of hand. Many sailors from the sunken schooner were buried in the small graveyard of St. Michael's church. Even two Frenchmen from the brigantine had been laid to rest there—much to the anger of some of the villagers. The vicar held his ground, however, and refused to be swayed by any of their threats.

My maid, Ellie, became more and more dear to me, for she—apart from the *Times* and my aunt's letters—was my only link with London. We would reminisce about life in the great city, although our lives there had been very different. And even though she had not seen it for over two years, London was just as beloved to her as it was to me.

"I wish me mother and father 'ad never moved down 'ere, your ladyship. I do believe all the fresh air of Cornwall has made me mother sick . . . !"

Amused by her statement, I had hidden a smile, for I knew how concerned she was about her mother—who did not seem to respond to any of the treatments or medicine the doctor in Falmouth prescribed. I let Ellie visit her each weekend, for I recalled how concerned I had been when my own mother was ill.

Letting her go was a sacrifice to me, however, for with Lord Penross away such a great deal of the time, I felt Ellie to be my only real ally in the house. Although I tentatively trusted Harris, the assistant coachman, and the young footman, Tom, I had to remind myself that Harris worked very closely with the morose Trigg and that Tom was Mrs. Dawson's son. And I distinctly distrusted both the coachman and the housekeeper. In fact, I often caught Mrs. Dawson whispering to Miss Marsden when I would come upon them unexpectedly in the nursery or in the hallways.

Lent was almost over, and soon Easter would be upon us. Elizabeth had had several fittings for her dress, and I was delighted to see the way Mrs. Johns had worked with the fine material. I hoped that Lord Penross would be pleased to see his daughter in such a pretty outfit. It would make its first appearance on Easter Sunday, when we all assembled in the hall to attend church.

The children had been most attentive as I had taught them concerning the Easter story, and for such a small child William was quite thoughtful in his questions.

"But why did God's Son have to die for us? Are we really all that bad, Aunt Charlotte?" His eyes looked into mine hopefully, wanting me to say, "Of course not." And when I told him that there was no one who could claim to be perfect, he shook his head and sighed. "I do try, but it is very hard. . . . Perhaps if I stopped jumping on my bed when Miss Marsden isn't looking . . . ?"

I assured him it was a start, but that only our Lord could take away all our leanings toward wanting to do wrongful things: Easter was a great opportunity for us all to really look at our lives and see how far short we came in the light of our Lord's perfection.

As I shared the familiar story with the children, I felt it lifting my own spirit. Perhaps, after all, there was mending ahead for my tattered faith.

Easter Sunday dawned, and everyone was up earlier than usual. Elizabeth had been to my room several times, bringing the new dress with her and primping before the long cheval mirror. Miss Marsden had frowned upon such behavior, and had already described the dress as being much too frivolous. "It is teaching her to think far more about her attire than the meaning of Easter, Lady Charlotte."

I had replied, "Easter is a time for rejoicing, and I see no harm in a child being able to express her faith in an outward expression of joy. If she were someone who did not understand nor care about the meaning of this great Church celebration, then I would be concerned. But Elizabeth has a deep faith and seems to realize the glorious meaning of our Lord's resurrection."

Elizabeth was the last one to walk down the vast staircase that morning. William had preceded her, looking almost cherubic in a navy-blue outfit complete with peaked cap. I must say, Elizabeth looked quite lovely. Even Lord Penross was proud and happy to see his daughter dressed so enchantingly, and applauded her with a broad smile upon his face. The small bright yellow bonnet, bedecked with yellow ribbons, and the high-necked ruffled dress, embroidered delicately with spring flowers, enhanced the young girl's coloring. For the first time I saw a really radiant expression upon her young face as she basked in her father's approval.

"Elizabeth, my dear, happy Easter. You seem to embody the joy we should all be feeling this morning." The dark mood that for weeks had weighed on Lord Penross seemed to lift momentarily. I breathed a sigh of relief.

He turned to me, and I sensed the appreciation he felt. "You have indeed made my daughter happy, Lady Charlotte. May I say how charming you look, also? Quite the perfect foil in your pale green."

I thanked him and heard a decided sniff of disapproval from Miss Marsden, who was standing behind me. My dress had been the latest fashion in London two years ago—here in Cornwall I realized it was still before its time. I had to admit I was grateful to France for the empire style that had become so popular. It had swept away the cumbersome hooped skirts and had brought with it a simplicity that was most becoming—and considerably easier to wear.

An open carriage awaited us outside the great front doors, and as I stepped out into one of the most beautiful sunlit mornings that I had experienced since arriving at Penross, I was thankful to our Lord for such a day. Good Friday had been dark and overcast; squalls had blown in from the sea, bringing stinging rain that had lashed Penross most of the day. But now the air smelled crisp and fresh, with the promise of uninterrupted sunshine—at least for a few hours. The gardens were a blaze of color, and as I looked down toward the sea before entering the carriage the scene was magnificent. Whitecaps, riding triumphantly on the brilliant blue water, fanned and disintegrated against the unyielding dark granite rocks. It was good to be in Cornwall on such a day.

I sat opposite Lord Penross and Elizabeth, with William beside me, and the carriage rolled down the steep driveway—the servants' carriage following not far behind.

I felt Lord Penross staring at me, and to escape his eyes I turned to watch the trees as they fluttered past us, their leaves joining overhead to form a green, lacy tunnel.

"Papa thinks you are very pretty, Aunt Charlotte—and so do I . . ."

William's words made me blush, and I felt most embarrassed. I kept my eyes averted until I was compelled to look in Lord Penross's direction. A faint smile hovered on his lips, and in his eyes I saw the affirmation of William's remark. I could see by Elizabeth's expression that the old hostility had returned.

"Thank you, William," I whispered, "but we must now concentrate on what this day means to all of us."

In the distance, the bells of St. Michael's were pealing their Easter welcome to one and all . . .

12

It was indeed a joyous service. Listening to the vicar deliver the Easter sermon helped me to find new hope from the meaning of the holy day.

As we were leaving the church, the vicar pressed a small, leatherbound book into my hands, whispering, "Perhaps John Wesley will encourage you, Lady Charlotte."

I looked down to see a collection of the great man's sermons. "I do thank you, Mr. Ashford. This will indeed be most interesting reading."

Lord Penross watched the exchange with a frown, a look of suspicion crossing his face.

Later that day, after a most delightful time with the children, I had gone to the library and sat reading Wesley's writings. The doors swung open, and I saw Lord Penross standing there. He paused for a few moments, taking in the fact that I was reading the book, then turned as if to leave.

"Did you wish to be alone in the library, Lord Penross? I can most easily continue reading in my room . . ."

"Pray do not move, Lady Charlotte. I have no wish to interrupt such laudable studies." I noted the sarcasm in his voice. Walking toward me, his hands behind his back, he said pointedly, "I witnessed something today that was truly unique."

"Oh, and what was that, Lord Penross?"

"The clergy bestowing a gift on one of its adoring donors.

Methinks the age of miracles is not passed after all. The vicar is usually asking for gifts—not giving them."

"The vicar merely wished to share the Reverend John Wesley's thoughts with me. His own life was greatly touched by them."

"Indeed." Lord Penross walked over to a large globe of the world and spun it quite forcefully. Watching the hemispheres rotate at a dizzying speed, he said quietly, "Then perhaps after you have been blessed by such inflammatory teachings, you will see to it that you do not in any way confuse my children. I expect them to remain true to the teachings of the Church of England."

He stopped the spinning globe with his index finger, and turned to glare down at me.

"I certainly respect that, Lord Penross, being a member of the Church myself. It is only that I wish to learn more, so that my faith can become infinitely stronger . . ."

"And you cannot find that through the established Church?"

"Quite possibly, but I have regretted a lack of warmth in my own experience, and I long to know what it was that Wesley and Reverend Ashford found . . ."

At the mention of the vicar's name, Lord Penross became incensed. "Ashford . . . Ashford! Are we to live and breathe by command of this man? He seems to have encroached into every part of our lives!"

Lord Penross strode out of the library, slamming the great doors behind him.

I sat quite amazed by the intensity of the feelings that the mild-mannered vicar had aroused.

Looking down at an open page of the offending book, I read, ". . . Let us do unto all, as we would they should do to us. Let us love and honour all men. Let justice, mercy, and truth govern all our minds and actions."

I could not help but smile, thinking how hard it seemed for Lord Penross to bestow these feelings on the vicar. But there was more than just an unreasonable anger toward Mr. Ashford on the part of Lord Penross. I sensed a deep frustration and a longing to know what I, too, was searching for . . . and did I detect a degree of jealousy? I put these thoughts from my mind and continued to read.

Nevertheless, thoughts of Lord Penross kept invading my time of study.

The following weeks seemed to bring a cold distance between Lord Penross and myself. He was polite, but I sensed an underlying impatience caused not only by me but by all the circumstances pertaining to the Penross estate.

The *Times* was filled with news of France—and Belgium, where the British and some of their allies were now entrenched. Napoleon had completed amassing a huge army. Even the Frenchmen who had turned against him, when they heard the call to arms from his impassioned lips, fell at his feet and declared themselves true to his cause. All Europe was in an uproar, waiting for the Emperor to strike.

A letter from Stephen divulged that General Wellington was continuing to rally our allies, the Germans and the Dutch, urging them to stand together. It would not be long before a great battle would ensue, and Stephen, no doubt, would be in the midst of it. How I longed to see him, and to know that he was safe.

At breakfast one morning, Lord Penross was absorbed as usual in the newspaper when he suddenly stood to his feet and uttered, "No! . . . oh, no!"

His face turned an ashen color, and I could see he was deeply distressed.

"Is it news concerning the war," I asked nervously.

Remembering my presence, he hastily replied, "No . . . nothing like that . . ." and left the room, taking the newspaper with him.

I was anxious to read whatever it was that had concerned him, but he obviously did not wish to discuss it. Nor did he leave the newspaper in the hall for me, as was his usual practice. Days went by without my coming across that edition of the *Times*.

One dismal morning a few weeks later, I had left my room to seek out William in the nursery. He was sitting at a table opposite Elizabeth, trying to fathom the seeming imponderables of mathematics—which he hated almost as much as Latin. Miss Marsden's frosty look toward me conveyed that

I was interrupting, and I turned to leave. But as I did so, I saw that the nurserymaid was having difficulty trying to kindle a fire.

I approached her and noticed a bundle of old newspapers in a basket by the fireplace.

"Here, let me help you. Perhaps if we hold one of these up to the opening of the grate it will help the fire to draw."

Miss Marsden immediately remarked that it was not seemly for me to be helping a nurserymaid. Paying no heed to her, I quickly unfolded several of the pages and knelt down beside the young girl.

"Oh, thank you, your ladyship," she said. "The wood must be damp—we've had nothing but rain for weeks."

We held the pages tightly across the opening, and it was while doing so that I noticed they were from the missing newspaper—the one I had been so anxious to read.

An article caught my eye, for I saw the word *Penross* in its title:

PENROSS KIN SIGHTED NEAR PENZANCE?

The Honorable Justin Penross, who escaped from the Launceston assizes two years ago, was reportedly seen in Penzance, Cornwall, recently. In 1813, he was accused of murdering his brother's wife, the Lady Caroline Penross, and sentenced to be hanged. Conspirators, however, were able to overpower his guards and help in his escape . . .

This was all I could read, for a scorchmark appeared on the paper, and within seconds it was enveloped in flames. I hastily picked up a fire iron and pushed the charred remains into the grate. It disintegrated and made its blackened way up the chimney, leaving behind a cloud of sparks and minute particles that proceeded to land upon my skirt. Brushing them off, I rose and hastily took a few steps backward. The fire was now burning brightly, and after the nurserymaid thanked me once more, I left the room . . . still astonished by what I had just read, and wishing I could have seen the whole article.

In the corridor, I looked down the long gallery toward the east wing and the Green Room. Puzzle pieces were beginning to come together in my mind. Was the Honorable Justin Penross hiding in this great house? Was it he whom I had encountered the night I went to get my Testament? (It would have been easy to have mistaken him in the moonlight for his brother.) There was the matter of the door in the paneling—and that terrible sensation that I was not alone in the chapel . . .

And always my thoughts returned to the sinister face looking down at me from the turret window!

A shiver ran through me as I remembered. I had to try to find out if my suspicions were correct. So, on the pretext of using the long gallery for its original purpose of exercise during inclement weather, I began walking toward the Green Room.

I was slowly making my way down the hallway stopping once or twice to examine a painting or a statue—even those dreaded suits of armor—when I suddenly encountered Mrs. Dawson. She was running her finger along the oak, linenfold paneling, testing to see whether it had been recently dusted. I did not wish to arouse her suspicions. Surely if Justin Penross was in hiding here, she must know and be part of the conspiracy.

Mrs. Dawson finally disappeared into the nursery, and I walked swiftly toward the Green Room door, putting my ear against it, listening for any sound that might tell me that there was someone in hiding.

A door behind me suddenly opened. For an instant I stood frozen, not able to move. Then I turned to see Rogers standing there.

"Rogers, how you startled me!" I tried to regain my composure.

"So I see, Lady Charlotte . . ."

His eyes were as cold as steel.

He held a large tray, upon which were several silver-covered dishes and a ewer of wine.

The silence between us was devastating. He offered no explanation as to the tray.

I began the long walk to my room, not daring to look back. When I finally did, Rogers was nowhere in sight.

13

*U*pon *entering my room, I felt a compelling desire to* confide my suspicions to someone. I was now more than ever convinced that the Honorable Justin Penross was in hiding—here, within the walls of Penross Manor.

But to whom could I turn? Lord Penross would not be returning for several days. Even so, I wondered if perhaps he knew that his brother was taking refuge here. I put my hands to my forehead—trying to quell the many disturbing thoughts that assailed me—and walked over to the window seat, and sat down, oblivious of the magnificent view before me.

I could not put the burden of my concerns upon Ellie, whose worries about her mother were beginning to wear on her. And I had my doubts about the other servants . . . how could they *not* know of someone living in the house?

It was then that the vicar's voice came back to me—that first Sunday morning I had met him. ". . . If I can ever be of help to you, in any way, please let me know, Lady Charlotte."

Of course! He was the only one I could trust.

I went over to the escritoire and, sitting down hastily, wrote the vicar a letter, asking that he call at Penross tomorrow morning at ten o'clock. I lit a taper and sealed the letter with my crest, then rang the bell for a servant.

But again—who could I trust? After pacing up and down for several minutes, I decided that there was nothing in the letter that could make anyone aware of my misgivings. There was a knock on the door, and I saw with gratitude that the young footman Tom had answered the bell.

Running my fingers over the seal once more to be certain it would hold, I asked, "Tom, would you please deliver this letter to the vicarage—if possible, to Mr. Ashford in person—and let me know of his reply?"

"Very good, m'lady—I'll take it right away for ye."

Upon closing the door, I had misgivings about my impulsive action—yet I could not keep to myself any longer my suspicions of what might be happening right here in this frightening house. I waited impatiently for Tom's return.

The small carriage clock had only just struck the hour when a light tap on my door made me call, "Enter!" It was the footman, back within half an hour.

"You must have ridden like the wind, Tom. You are back so soon . . ."

"Anything for m'lady. I took the shortcut through the graveyard . . . talk about fearsome at dusk—all them tombstones. Makes a body wonder if 'e'll see a ghost or some such . . ." His eyes widened at the thought.

"Nonsense, Tom. There's no such thing as ghosts," I said, laughingly.

"Well, perhaps not where you're from, m'lady. But 'ere in Cornwall they're *everywhere.* We're mighty afear'd of ghosts. I could tell ye stories that would make yer blood curdle . . ."

Hastily changing the subject, I asked, "Did you find the vicar at home, Tom?"

"Indeed I did, m'lady, and 'e said 'e would be 'appy to grant your request—whatever that was . . ." He looked at me, as if expecting that I would tell him.

"Thank you, Tom, that will be all." I hastily drew the conversation to a close, thankful that Mr. Ashford would be visiting me tomorrow.

After Tom left, I wondered at the propriety of my asking the vicar to call, when my visiting him at the vicarage and even talking to him at church had raised Lord Penross's ire. However, it was too late to remedy my impetuous action. And I was anxious for ten o'clock tomorrow morning to arrive.

I dressed in a blue-gray, high-necked muslin dress for the vicar's visit—feeling it was appropriately decorous and could in no way be criticized by any of the servants.

The weather was spectacular that morning. The sun—apparent at dawn, without a hint of sea mist—made me decide to meet the vicar in the sunken Italian garden. Besides, I feared that wherever we met in the house, we were in danger of being overheard.

As soon as the church bells could be heard chiming ten o'clock, I walked to the garden—noticeably carrying the volume of John Wesley's sermons which the vicar had lent me. The flowers, growing in such profusion in this area of the grounds were splendid in the sunlight; the herbaceous borders a riot of color. As I nervously waited for the vicar, I recalled another garden I had known, at my family's country estate. But all the time I was uncomfortably conscious of the great house's watching eyes . . .

A few minutes after the hour, I heard the sound of a horse's hoofs. I looked back at the house, trying to look nonchalant, but fearing someone might suspect my reason for meeting with the vicar. Shortly afterward, in the distance, I saw him riding toward me. The white tabs of his clerical collar fluttered in the light sea breeze, and his black, wide-brimmed hat hid part of his face from me. It was not until Mr. Ashford dismounted, tied his horse, and walked quickly down the steps to where I was sitting, that I could see he was most concerned.

"Lady Charlotte, I beg your forgiveness for being late. There were some unforeseen church matters I had to attend to . . ."

"You are indeed forgiven, Mr. Ashford. I used the time to appreciate once more the beauty of this garden. There are so many different flowers. Unfortunately, I do not know all their names . . ." And we spent a few moments in polite pleasantries, I all the while wondering how I would broach my subject.

As we slowly walked around the flower beds, I found it difficult to concentrate on what the vicar was saying. I was certain that if I looked toward the house now, I would see someone staring down at us. When I finally did look, a curtain in the library window moved, as if a hand had been holding it back.

The vicar's voice made me turn to him. "I see you have John Wesley's book with you—I trust you have found it to be interesting, as well as inspiring?"

"Oh, yes, indeed," I answered with feeling, "I believe I'm beginning more clearly to understand many facets concerning my faith."

I had placed a bookmark at a passage that had enlightened me, and showed the vicar. He took the book from me and began to read: "Through faith . . . [the believer] perceives the presence of Him in whom he lives, and moves, and has his being, and feels the love of God shed abroad in his heart. It is the internal evidence of Christianity . . ."

Mr. Ashford stopped reading and looked down at me, saying, "Ah, yes, that's the difference! To have the knowledge that He is with us in whatever circumstances we find ourselves—*and* that we are loved by Him."

"At times, I really do seem to sense that, Mr. Ashford—although I must also confess to times of doubt."

The vicar looked thoughtfully at me for a moment. "So must we all confess," he said quietly, then continued, "Wesley said that he regarded all the world as his parish. I'm glad that almost twenty-five years after his death, his books can still illuminate the reader, wherever he—or *she*—happens to be."

The vicar smiled and, closing the book, handed it back to me.

"Mr. Ashford, I feel I have kept it long enough. You surely may be needing it?"

" 'Twas a gift to you, Lady Charlotte." He saw me start to refuse. "No, I insist. It brings me great joy to be able to share Wesley's thoughts with another . . ."

I thanked him profusely, and we began to walk toward the house. I realized he must have thought my request to see him was to return his book. I felt foolish, for I did not quite know how to transfer the conversation from such a high plane to one which he might regard as the product of a young woman's overactive imagination.

"Mr. Ashford . . . there was another matter I wished to

discuss. It may seem absurd, but, nevertheless, I feel compelled to share it with you."

"By all means, Lady Charlotte." He could see I was distressed. "You know that you have my confidence."

I turned my back upon the house, and we proceeded to walk once more around the sunken garden.

Not knowing quite how to begin, I found myself blurting out, "I believe there is someone hiding within the walls of Penross Manor!" The vicar's glance involuntarily turned to the house, but I spoke quickly: "Do not let your actions betray what we are discussing—I fear we are being watched."

"Lady Charlotte, what has made you believe there is someone in hiding?" And then I told him the occurrences behind my growing suspicions.

When I had finished, Mr. Ashford walked beside me, his head down, deep in thought. "There could be rational explanations for all these occurrences. An old manor house such as Penross develops many strange noises over the years. The face you saw could have been a shadow caused by the lightning; and, possibly, Lord Penross did return that night. Then, the lack of proper ventilation in some of our old chapels could have made you feel apprehensive, Lady Charlotte."

"Then how do you explain the tray that Rogers was carrying? None of the rooms in the east wing are occupied." I anxiously awaited his reply.

With complete seriousness, the vicar looked at me and inquired, "Could it be that Rogers was having a secret party?"

I went to answer him and then saw that his eyes were twinkling. The thought of the stiff, frowning Rogers being involved in a secret revel made me throw my head back and laugh, and the vicar joined me.

I replied, "I sometimes wonder—poor man—if Rogers has ever really known what it is to laugh and, even for a few moments, experience pleasure."

"God gave us laughter, Lady Charlotte—'A merry heart doeth good like a medicine.' We do not avail ourselves often enough of its recuperative powers."

I sighed, imagining myself back in the warmth of my

family home. "Oh, how I miss the times of laughter when I was with my dear family. I took so much for granted then—thinking we would always be together . . ."

I could see a shadow of sadness in his eyes, also. "As we grow older, those memories become more and more dear to us, Lady Charlotte. I certainly find that is true of me." Then, bringing us back to the subject, he asked, "Is there anything else that has led you to believe there could possibly be someone in hiding?"

I thought about the newspaper account of Justin Penross. "Mr. Ashford—if he *has* come back to Penross, is it not my duty to inform the constabulary?"

"It would be, Lady Charlotte, but I fear you have not enough evidence to prove your suspicions. Have you shared your fears with Lord Penross?"

"No. I could not bring myself to—you are the only person in whom I have confided."

"Then, let us keep it secret for the present, and I will do all I can to find out what latest news, if any, the constabulary has of the Honorable Justin's whereabouts. It could be that your assumptions are correct, Lady Charlotte—but they could also be a plausible misconception."

We were nearing the steps leading up to the driveway when I heard in the distance the sound of horses' hoofs. Then, a short time later, Lord Penross's carriage came into view. Trigg was sitting up front, cracking his whip and urging the horses onward. The four magnificent white horses strained against their harnesses as if the sight of home gave them an added burst of energy, then came to a snorting stop outside the front door. Trigg quickly climbed down to open the carriage door for Lord Penross.

He had already seen us from afar, and showed no sign of surprise as he alighted. "Well, well, the vicar is making a parochial call, I see."

I walked toward the carriage and smiled. "Welcome home, Lord Penross."

"As always, it is good to be home. Perhaps I should not leave it quite so often." He looked down at me, a quizzical expression on his face.

"I am sure we all feel that way, Lord Penross." I glanced quickly at the vicar. "Mr. Ashford was just leaving . . ."

"Ah, yes, I was saying my farewells. I trust all is well with you, Lord Penross."

Lord Penross curtly nodded and began to walk up the steps. While his back was turned, I said goodbye to Mr. Ashford; when I proferred my hand, he took it and whispered, "Take heart, Lady Charlotte—I will be in contact with you."

Lord Penross swung round before entering the house and watched the vicar leave.

"Come, Lady Charlotte, I am anxious to see the children and to hear from you all they have learned during my absence."

"I was about to go and meet them in the music room. They have a special surprise for you."

I was acutely conscious of his presence beside me as we walked down the long, dark corridor leading to the music room. He opened the door and stood aside to let me pass; my hand brushed his as I entered.

"Pray forgive me, Lord Penross . . ."

"Charmed, I am sure, Lady Charlotte."

I looked up to see him smiling and hurriedly walked over to the pianoforte—wishing the children would arrive for their lesson, yet enjoying the excitement that seemed to grow each time I found myself in his presence.

14

The children were now several minutes late. I walked over to the window and made a pretense of seeing whether they were in the garden. There was an awkward silence. I wished to ask him about his brother, but as I turned to him he requested I play the pianoforte.

I chose Beethoven's "Moonlight Sonata"—its drama helping to alleviate my self-consciousness. Lord Penross leaned over the pianoforte and watched my hands as they flew up and down the keyboard. I felt as if at any moment he would reach out and touch me . . .

My hand slipped, and I played a wrong note.

I looked up at him, and he laughed in mock surprise. "Lady Charlotte, I did not think you capable of such a transgression!"

"I must not have been completely concentrating, Lord Penross."

We both laughed, and he was about to speak when the children came into the music room. I was relieved, yet at the same time almost wishing our time alone could have been longer . . .

"Bonjour, Papa," the children cried in unison, happy to see that their father had returned—and to show off their newly learned French. They ran to him for an embrace, then Lord Penross asked if they would play a duet for him. The children needed no more encouragement. William picked up his flute, while Elizabeth exchanged places with me at the pianoforte.

"Papa, you are really going to be surprised when you hear what we have learned." William looked over at Elizabeth, and together they began to play a simple folk tune I had arranged for them.

They played it sweetly, if not faultlessly, and were encouraged by Lord Penross's exuberant praise.

"Splendid, children. I have now been blessed by hearing two exquisitely played pieces of music." Turning to me, he said, "Lady Charlotte, you are not only a superb pianist, but also a gifted teacher."

"Thank you, Lord Penross, but your children have a natural aptitude—it is easy to teach them."

"Then let us hear more of this newly found talent."

William whispered to Elizabeth, who nodded, and they began to play a Shakespearean song that I had taught them. As they came to the end, Lord Penross cried, "Encore!" and proceeded to sing the words:

> It was a lover and his lass,
> With a hey, and a ho, and a hey nonino . . .

Lord Penross's pleasingly resonant tenor voice filled the music room. He beckoned me to sing with him, and the children continued to play. I sang hesitantly at first—wishing that I had taught them any other song but this one, for Lord Penross's eyes seemed to pull at mine, and once more I felt this growing awareness between us.

> That o'er the green cornfield did pass,
> In spring time, the only pretty ring time,
> When birds do sing, hey ding a ding, ding;
> Sweet lovers love the spring.

Lord Penross applauded once more. "Enchanting, quite enchanting, children. And, Lady Charlotte, might I say you have a particularly delightful soprano voice. I believe it was trained for more than the occasional family gathering."

"I have often sung in recitals given by my aunt. But that has not been for some time now . . ."

"We shall have to remedy that. Penross Manor needs to be opened once more for social gatherings." His face beamed. I had never seen him quite so animated.

"Children, you will have to add more to your repertoire; then you, too, shall be a part of the program."

William was excited about such a proposal. However, Elizabeth—who had been watching the repartee between Lord Penross and myself—acted indifferent. Her mouth was set in a determined line. I wondered if there had been musical evenings in which her mother was the featured artiste.

The gong sounded for luncheon, and the children—asking to be excused—scampered out of the room. Punctuality was stressed by Miss Marsden, and I had no doubt that she was already waiting for them at the top of the great staircase.

"I'm feeling quite famished myself after the long drive. Come, Lady Charlotte; during luncheon I hope you will enlighten me as to all the latest news—especially that which pertains to your church work . . ."

I looked up at him, wondering if, in spite of the light banter that had gone on in the music room, he was still troubled by seeing me with the vicar in the garden. It was not an easy task to sense his moods accurately. I felt he would be angry, indeed, if he knew of my conversation with the vicar concerning his brother, Justin.

But luncheon proved to be a pleasant meal, and Lord Penross seemed to express genuine interest in the affairs of the village, and the great needs that still had to be met amongst the villagers. There was still no sign of finding any new tin lode in the mines.

"God has not chosen to answer your prayers as yet, Lady Charlotte."

"Then we must keep praying, Lord Penross." I looked him directly in the eye, knowing he was trying to deride my beliefs. But in truth, I had begun to wonder whether my prayers concerning the dire needs of the Penross miners were of any avail.

It was during dessert that Rogers came in bearing a silver salver, upon which was a note for me from the vicar. I asked Lord Penross if he would excuse me whilst I read it.

The tinge of sarcasm crept back in his voice as he responded: "Never let it be said that I in any way impeded progress between you and the . . . Church." But his sarcasm vanished when he saw my face upon reading the note. The vicar had written to tell me that Mrs. Johns, the seamstress, had been imprisoned, and to ask me to visit her as early as was convenient.

When I shared this news with Lord Penross, he immediately rang for Rogers and asked for Harris to bring the carriage to the front door. Ellie was summoned to accompany me, and Mrs. Dawson instructed to pack a small hamper of food.

"Tell her we will do all we can to help her and her children." I was gratified by Lord Penross's concern.

Outside, the sky was beginning to cloud over, and I was glad of my pelisse and bonnet. In the comfort of the elegant carriage, I thought of the dreadful conditions in which Mrs. Johns now found herself.

The carriage came to a stop outside the vile building used to house prisoners. Ellie and I walked up to the heavily barred door and tugged at the bell, and after a few minutes I could hear the jailer turn the great key and the door swung open. "Well, well, 'tis her ladyship, come to spread a little 'appiness . . ." He leered at me, and I could smell whiskey upon his breath.

"Do not be insolent with me. I come here at the express wish of Lord Penross to see Mrs. Johns." My knees were shaking, but my voice sounded authoritative.

At the mention of the name of Penross, the jailer's expression changed. "But of course, yer ladyship. Follow me . . ." and he falteringly walked in front of Ellie and me down the dank, oppressive corridor which led to the communal cell for women I had visited several times now. He fumbled for the key. Finally, the filthy door opened, and the stench of human beings left to rot in their own excrement assailed us.

A perfumed handkerchief to my nose was a poor defense against the odor, and Ellie looked about to faint.

It was then that I spotted Mrs. Johns. She was chained to the wall, sitting with her head in her rough hands, trying to ignore the noise and squalor on either side of her.

"Mrs. Johns, I've come to see you . . ."

A pockmarked woman crouched on the floor mimicked my words, then broke into shrill gales of laughter. Several other prisoners followed suit, taunting me, and others shouted obscenities.

I spoke to Mrs. Johns again, but she did not seem to hear me. Then she looked up, bewildered, and tried in the half-light to make out who stood before her. Finally, I saw a look of recognition.

"Yer ladyship! Oh, God bless ye for comin'." Tears ran down her cheeks. "I'm so worried about the children. I never 'ad time to tell me sister to take care of 'em . . . even though she's just right next door. The constables just came and searched me 'ouse, and then took me away . . ."

I promised to look after them, then asked her why she had been imprisoned.

"They said they found contraband in me 'ouse, but all it was was a bolt o' red silk, wot Lady Penross 'ad given me years ago. I 'ad been keeping it for when me daughters were older, so I could make 'em a fancy gown . . ."

"Does anyone else know that Lady Penross gave it to you? Would Lord Penross . . . ?"

She dejectedly shook her head. "We was alone when she gave it to me. The silk was left over from when I made 'er a dress, for when she sat for 'er portrait." Then she said with more animation, "I wore that very same dress the day I came to Penross Manor—the day I first met ye. You know, when I came to measure Mistress Elizabeth for 'er Easter outfit."

I did indeed remember the tattered, faded dress, and had wondered then where she could possibly have obtained it.

"Why did Lady Penross give it to you?"

"She grew tired of the dress, me lady. After she wore it for 'er portrait, she felt as if everyone would always recognize it. . . . It's been over six years now . . ."

I wondered if Mrs. Johns was telling me the truth. "I have never seen a portrait of Lady Penross."

"No, I 'spect not. After Lady Penross was—well—after she died, Lord Penross took it from the great 'all and 'ung it in 'is bedchamber."

"Then, Mrs. Johns, I will request the head constable to come to Penross and see the portrait for himself. Is the dress in your cottage?"

"It should be. That's if no one 'as stolen it. I left it 'anging in the cupboard under the stairs . . ."

"I will go from here and see if I can find it. Also, I shall see whether your sister has taken charge of the children."

"Bless ye, m'lady."

"Mrs. Johns, I've brought you some food." Ellie, who had been standing nervously behind me, spoke up, handing the basket to Mrs. Johns. Immediately the women on either side of her began to claw at the basket cover, reaching inside.

" 'Tis good of ye, yer ladyship, but I can't eat—not with worryin' . . ."

I gave some of the food to the half-crazed women, but insisted Mrs. Johns eat something. She made a half-hearted attempt. "Try, try to eat. We'll do everything to get you out of here, but you've got to keep strong, Mrs. Johns."

"I will try, knowing ye are 'elping me. Give me love to my younguns, won't ye?" At the mention of her children, she began to cry.

With tears in my own eyes, I bent to embrace her. "I'll give them your message. Do not give up hope, Mrs. Johns. You are not alone, even here in this prison. Our Lord is with you . . ."

Even though by now most of the women were screaming and taunting us, I managed to pray with Mrs. Johns. She clutched my hand and thanked me for coming, just as the jailer stuck in his head and suggested it was time to leave.

Once outside in the fresh air, I took a deep breath, relieved to be away from such a loathsome place, but heartsick about leaving Mrs. Johns there. I gave orders to Harris to drive to the seamstress's cottage, which was near the wharf in a very seedy, run-down part of the village.

"Are you sure, m'lady?"

"Quite . . ." and asked that he be as quick as possible.

The front door of the ramshackle cottage was ajar. Entering, I saw how dilapidated the tiny dwelling still was, even though the church had made some endeavor to help Mrs. Johns. The two small rooms downstairs were furnished with just the absolute necessities.

I found the faded dress where Mrs. Johns had said it would be and quickly took it off the hook, handing it to

Ellie. Then I went to the cottage next door, where Mrs. Johns had said her sister lived. The woman who answered the door bore a remarkable resemblance.

I introduced myself and asked if the children were with her.

"That they are, poor mites. They're downright frightened—what with their father gone, and now their mother . . ."

I assured her that everything was being done to obtain Mrs. Johns's release and gave her some money to help take care of the children, promising to return the next day. Then I urged Harris to drive to Penross as fast as was possible. I had to see for myself that there really was a portrait of Lady Penross in a red silk dress.

Once at the manor house, I took the dress from Ellie and raced up the staircase. Observing that the gallery was deserted, I quickly walked toward Lord Penross's room and knocked, but there was no answer.

I hesitated. But then, impelled both by concern for Mrs. Johns and my own curiosity, I turned the handle and threw open the door.

There before me, hanging resplendent in an elaborate gilt frame between two great windows overlooking the sea, was a full-length portrait of Lady Penross. There was no doubt it was she—I could see the likeness to William in her eyes, and in the color of her luxuriant fair hair.

The dress she wore *was* the faded, tattered one I now held in my hands. But in the portrait it was magnificent. The brilliant red silk shone as it clung to the softly rounded form. The sweeping skirt fanned down to the matching shoes, and delicate lace framed her face and hands . . .

"She was beautiful, was she not?"

Lord Penross's voice made me swing round.

He was standing behind me—a haunted look in his eyes.

I whispered, "Yes, she was very beautiful . . ."

We stood looking up at the portrait for what seemed like hours, but could only have been several melancholy moments.

15

The head constable was summoned and shown the evidence of the old, tattered dress and the portrait. At first, there was doubt that the dress was made from the same bolt of red silk that had been confiscated from Mrs. Johns's cottage—or that it could possibly be the same one Lady Penross wore in the painting. But I tore open the hem of the old dress showing the man the vivid original color that had not faded, and the head constable finally agreed there had been a mistake. He said that Mrs. Johns would be released immediately.

"I trust you will make restitution to her," Lord Penross said harshly. "The woman has gone through far too much harassment. Also, I understand conditions at the jail have not been improved as I recommended . . ."

The head constable bowed several times, assuring Lord Penross that he had given orders to see that the jail was "put to rights" and that he would look into the matter once more. With further assurances of seeing that Mrs. Johns was taken to her cottage without any more ado and with regrets for the error of his men, the head constable hastily left the manor.

Lord Penross and I walked together into the dining hall. I still felt embarrassed about having opened his bedchamber door—even for a worthy reason. I had apologized, but nevertheless I felt as if I had intruded into a very personal part of his life. And I felt I would never forget the sound of his pensive, "She was beautiful . . ."

I steeled myself to realize that any feelings I was nurturing for this handsome, enigmatic man must be put aside; he was clearly still possessed by the memory of his beautiful, tragic wife. I was almost convinced now that he had had no part in Lady Caroline's murder. Yet the smallest doubt continued to nag at me, for men have been known to destroy even those they hold most dear. . . .

At dinner Lord Penross was silent, and I could see the haunted, brooding mood had now entirely enveloped him. And the next day he left Penross Manor, saying he would be gone for several weeks. He was always evasive as to where he was going, or what he did on all of his trips. "Business to attend to" was the only information I had ever obtained.

Now, once more, I faced the loneliness of the house, and the suspicion that the murderer, Justin Penross, was living beneath the same roof. I longed to admit my suspicions to the proper authorities, but I held back because of the vicar's advice and a feeling I should talk first to Lord Penross about the matter.

I was grateful that there was much to do. I oversaw the restoration of Mrs. Johns's and her sister's cottages. (Mrs. Johns had refused an invitation to live at Penross, claiming she would be out of place there and feel much more at home in the little house to which she was accustomed.)

I also concentrated on Elizabeth and William. They had been introduced to Latin, French, and now a little German, and they were making astounding progress.

Elizabeth continued to be cool towards me, although there were signs of a future thaw. After seeing Lady Penross's portrait, I had mentioned to Elizabeth what a beautiful woman their mother had been. Elizabeth had looked at me— a challenging expression upon her face.

"No one could *ever* take her place."

"I am sure that is true, Elizabeth. No matter who comes into our lives, even if we grow to love them, they can never be a substitute for someone we have lost—for God has created each one of us differently. However, I believe He does allow the love of others to help heal the loss."

Elizabeth did not respond, but I saw tears shining in her

eyes, before she brusquely turned away from me and left the room.

It was early one morning in June that I was awakened to the incessant sound of the church bells tolling. Half-asleep, I got out of bed and ran to the window. Several people were excitedly milling about the driveway.

My first reaction was that perhaps the French had invaded—or even the Americans, whose ships had been sighted several times—and the likelihood of bombardment was feared. But all was quiet, except for the tolling of the bells and the sound of voices in the driveway.

I wrapped my dressing gown around me and opened the bedchamber door, just as Ellie was about to knock.

"M'lady—such news—" She was trying to get her breath.

"Then tell me, Ellie, please do . . ."

"It's Napoleon! 'E's been defeated! At Waterloo! A ship arrived at Falmouth during the night with the news!"

I could scarcely believe my ears. "Ellie, is it true?" We were crying and laughing at the same time.

She wiped her eyes and nodded. "Oh, yes, it's true all right. Everyone is talking about it. Old Boney is in retreat. I 'ope when they catch 'im, they lock 'im up better than wot they did last time. We don't want no little Emperor doing a bunk off anuvver island . . ."

While she rattled on, I was thinking of my brother, Stephen—of what this news meant concerning him. Had he been in the midst of the great battle? Was he safe? When would I hear news of him? Letters had stopped several weeks ago, and I had hoped that meant only that he was unable to correspond because of security reasons.

The door to the nursery burst open, and William rushed into the gallery. "What's all the noise about, Aunt Charlotte?"

"Napoleon has been defeated at Waterloo, William! It seems the war will soon be over."

He ran to me and flung his arms around my waist. "Oh, Aunt Charlotte! How did you find out?"

Ellie told him that a ship had docked in Falmouth with the news.

His eyes lit up. "Could we go there today?"

I hesitated. It was a long drive, and Lord Penross was not home to give his permission.

"Please, oh, please, Aunt Charlotte!" William jumped up and down with excitement. "When news came of the victory at Trafalgar, they had all kinds of parades in Falmouth—there were so many ships in the harbor. . . . I've always wished I could've been there."

Ellie chimed in, "Oh, yes, yer ladyship. I saw it all. It was ever so exciting!"

Two sets of eyes were pleading with me. I thought of all the reasons why we should not go—and then—impulsively—said, "Very well. But you have to promise me, William, that you will write an essay on what you see today." His nose wrinkled up. "You will be missing a great deal of school time."

"Very well, I promise, Aunt Charlotte. I'll go and tell Elizabeth." He went to the nursery door, then stopped and looked back. "But what about Miss Marsden?" His face had now taken on a glum expression.

"Leave her to me, William."

Convincing Miss Marsden as to the propriety of the journey to Falmouth proved to be most difficult. I finally told her that I would take all responsibility concerning it—and why did she not come, too? After all, it would be history enacted before us.

Miss Marsden narrowed her eyes and drew herself up indignantly. "I would sooner read about the event, Lady Charlotte, than be subject to the kind of element that will be out in the streets. I am surprised you would think it a fit place for the children."

"They are confined in this house far too much, Miss Marsden. The trip will be most educational for them . . ."

At first Elizabeth, obviously concerned that Miss Marsden did not approve, refused to go with us. But William insisted, pulling at her hand.

"Come on, Elizabeth—we can leave our old lessons for one day!" he whispered.

She reluctantly gave in, and arrangements were made for the journey. The young coachman, Harris, was informed, a hamper was packed with food and drinks, and an hour later we set out for Falmouth.

111

The journey proved to be quite exhausting—the roads being heavily rutted by constant use—but the thought of seeing the celebrations kept all of us in a mood of happy anticipation. Even Elizabeth forgot her usual air of reluctance and spent the time pointing out different places of interest. Ellie was in a state of bliss; not only would she see the parade, she would be able to visit her family and be with her mother for an hour or so.

We reached Falmouth by noon and dropped off Ellie at her family's cottage just as cannons from Pendennis Castle were firing a salute to the great victory. People of all descriptions good-naturedly jostled each other in the streets. There were many open carriages bearing gentlemen and ladies in fine apparel, and we all lined up on the wharf to wait for the parade. The noise of the crowd reminded me of London, and I realized how much I missed seeing other people. It was good to feel a part of something exciting again.

The harbor was choked with ships and small boats—all flying flags and sounding their sirens to add to the excitement of the merrymaking. Children, with wreaths of flowers in their hair, danced in the street, and some threw flowers into the crowd. William and Elizabeth caught some blossoms and proceeded to decorate the interior of our open carriage. The sun beat down on us relentlessly, and I was glad of my parasol. Both children were hungry, so out came the hamper, and there in our carriage we picnicked on chicken, gingerbread, and large, luscious strawberries—toasting the military victory with sweet Cornish apple juice.

At last the militia marched by, splendid in their dress uniforms. The brass on their jackets and helmets shone in the sunshine, and the rousing music of their bands stirred the atmosphere.

But the sight and sounds of the military caused me to wonder about Stephen's whereabouts. Why hadn't I heard from him? Even amid all the noise of celebration, I had a strange sense of foreboding.

Now wagons filled with musicians were being pulled through the crowds by reluctant horses. People began to dance to the music. The children clapped their hands in time, and Elizabeth's face was ecstatic.

"Oh, I'm so glad we came, Aunt Charlotte. I've never seen anything like this before."

She did not realize she had called me "aunt," and I did not point it out for her. But it was the most festive moment of the day for me.

Later, a sailor went by with a brightly colored, large, red parrot on his shoulder, and once more the children were enthralled. He disappeared into a large crowd that had gathered near the wharf.

Then I had a shock of recognition: "Why, children, your father . . ."

My first reaction was that a tall man standing half-hidden in a dark doorway of one of the warehouses, a hat pulled down over his eyebrows, was Lord Penross. I looked again, but now I questioned whether it was he. The man was looking directly at me—a strange expression on his face. He did not come over to greet us.

The children distracted me, asking excitedly where I had seen their father—"No, no, I was mistaken . . ."

I looked once more toward the warehouse, but the man had vanished. My first instinct was to leave, and I told the coachman we must now be on our way. I told the protesting children we had miles to go, and it would be late afternoon before we arrived back at Penross.

I instructed Harris to go to Ellie's cottage and pick her up. As the carriage rolled away from the wharf, I hastily looked over at the warehouse once more, but could see no sign of the tall, mysterious man I had momentarily mistaken for Lord Penross.

Then I went icy cold, even though the sun was shining brilliantly. Leaning back in the carriage, I had closed my eyes and seen in my mind the face that had looked down at me from the turret my first night at Penross.

The man I had seen today and the one in the turret— they were one and the same!

16

"'Tis a day to remember! Three cheers for the Old King and 'Prinny'!"

Ellie's reference to George III and the Prince Regent made Elizabeth and William laugh and shout at the top of their voices. Ellie was in high spirits during the journey back to Penross. She rejoiced that her mother's health was much improved, and the excitement of the celebrations in Falmouth caused her to reminisce about other celebrations she had witnessed when living in London. The children were greatly entertained by her stories—for which I was grateful. I myself was still deeply troubled by the man I had seen at the wharf . . .

The roads were badly congested with other carriages leaving Falmouth, and it took us far longer than anticipated to reach Penross Manor. It was dusk when we turned into the driveway, and I saw that we were most fortunate to be home, for a storm was rolling in from the sea. The first drops of rain fell as we climbed from the carriage. The children ran ahead of me, laughing and still talking about what they had seen.

The candelabra were lit in the hall, casting shadows on the glistening, white-marble walls. I reflected as I had many times on what a magnificent entry it was to the manor.

At the top of the great, sweeping staircase, however, I was surprised to see the irate figure of Lord Penross. He was clenching both lapels of his black velvet jacket and angrily looking down at us.

"Papa, you're home. Oh, Papa, we've seen the most exciting sights today . . . !" William, unaware of how angry his father was, raced up the stairs to greet him.

Lord Penross stared at me. "Where, pray tell me, Lady Charlotte, did you take my children? I could scarcely believe Miss Marsden when she informed me you had all gone to Falmouth . . ."

His voice echoed through the great hall, and I felt as if all the servants must be able to hear him—even those whose tasks took them to the attics, or the basement. I saw Miss Marsden lurking in the darkness of the gallery, and Rogers made a pretence of straightening one of the family portraits.

"It was a most glorious day, Lord Penross. We were able to join in the celebrations which marked the victory of our troops over the French at Waterloo. I am sorry you missed it . . ." I kept my voice steady and polite, trying to control my annoyance; I realized Miss Marsden must have delighted in overdramatizing the hazards to which I had subjected the children by taking them on such a journey.

"Papa, it was a wonderful day . . . please don't be cross." I was surprised to hear Elizabeth's voice. "I shall never forget it." She ran up the staircase to her father and put her hand in his. "Lady Charlotte took great care of us." She reached up and kissed him, then looked down at me. "Thank you again."

Elizabeth ran along the gallery to the nursery. She was followed by William, who first blew me a kiss, then winked through the balustrade. I could not help but laugh, which seemed to annoy Lord Penross even more. He slowly walked down the stairs and stood towering over me.

"I fail to see the humor, Lady Charlotte. I was desperately worried concerning the children's and your safety."

"Please forgive me, Lord Penross. I am not trying to belittle your anxiety. William blew me a kiss before he left. His expressive face often causes me to laugh. He is like a ray of sunshine in an often-gloomy house."

I took off my bonnet and handed it to Ellie, who had been hovering in the background, obviously worried about the mood of her master.

"Why do we not go into the drawing room, Lord Penross, and I can inform you of all we saw today?"

I did not wait for his answer, but walked ahead, and upon entering the room exclaimed, "Are you not thankful indeed to know that Napoleon is in retreat? Perhaps soon we can all breathe a sigh of relief, and England will once more return to normal."

Lord Penross walked over to the fireplace, and I saw a smile begin to form. "Lady Charlotte, I am indeed thankful. I am thankful, too, for your being here. I feel the same as you do about William; he is a ray of sunshine in an otherwise gloomy house. But you are, too. Forgive me for being so angry. When I returned to find you and the children gone, I was much distressed. I sensed what this house would be like without you all . . ."

I was deeply touched by Lord Penross's open confession of such private feelings. Once again, he had surprised me. I had never known anyone who could be so angry one moment, and the next so contrite and candid. Repressing a desire to go to him, I walked over to the window and watched the rain streaming down the panes, blurring the view of the parkland at twilight.

"I know how you must have felt, Lord Penross. I, too, have been experiencing feelings of dread this day."

"Pray tell me why, Lady Charlotte."

"While all the celebrating was going on, my thoughts were of my brother Stephen. I know he must have been at Waterloo; his last letter intimated that the Coldstream Guards would be in the forefront of any battlefield. I have prayed so fervently for his safety, but I have a strange feeling all is not well." I bit my lip, not wanting to break down in front of Lord Penross.

"Then you must continue to have faith, Lady Charlotte. You have been a shining example to me since you have been here. Mine was shattered, I fear, when Lady Penross was . . ." He could not form the word *murdered*.

"I can understand; I, too, have experienced great doubts since my mother's death. But since reading John Wesley's writings . . ." I saw Lord Penross turn away. "Oh, I know you do not approve of him, but he has been most helpful to me. He speaks so eloquently concerning the hope that comes from our Lord's resurrection . . ."

Lord Penross looked down at the fireplace, and began to recite quietly:

> What can this Gospel of Jesus be?
> What Life and Immortality,
> What was it that he brought to Light
> That Plato & Cicero did not write?

Awed by the leading questions the words raised, I whispered, "What, indeed." I asked, "Who is the poet?—I don't recognize . . ."

"William Blake. I'm reading a collection of his latest poems; a friend in London recommended them. I find them most thought provoking."

The gong sounded for dinner, and I realized I had not changed my attire.

"Please excuse me, Lord Penross. I will only be a few minutes; then I will join you in the dining hall."

"Of course, Lady Charlotte. We can continue our conversation there."

I raced up the stairs, my emotions almost at a breaking point. I felt closer to Lord Penross than I had on any other occasion.

Perhaps tonight I could talk to him about his brother.

In spite of my feelings of concern regarding Stephen, dinner was a most pleasant meal. Lord Penross reminisced about the children's escapades prior to my coming to Penross, and I sensed a closeness—perhaps a feeling of true friendship—developing between us.

It was not until after dinner was finished and we were walking toward the library, that I felt equipped with the courage to broach the subject of the Honorable Justin Penross. We sat down facing each other on either side of the fireplace in the library, and I felt the time had come to mention the man I had seen in Falmouth.

"A rather curious thing happened this afternoon, Lord Penross."

"Oh, and what was that?" He replied rather absentmindedly as he leafed through a book that had newly arrived from London.

"I saw a man watching our carriage today—a man whom I felt I had seen before."

He now gave me his full attention. "What did he look like, Lady Charlotte?"

"At first I thought he was you, but then I realized I was mistaken."

"You say you have seen him before?"

"Yes, the night I arrived here at Penross—during that violent storm. Someone was watching from the eastern tower. I saw him for only a moment, but I am sure the expression on his face was identical to the man's in Falmouth."

Lord Penross rose and walked thoughtfully up and down the room.

"Lady Charlotte, I think you must be mistaken about seeing someone in the eastern tower. It—as well as the whole of the east wing—has been closed for several years. Of course, it is possible that a servant may have been attending to a window latch that had become loosened by the storm."

"I have not seen any servant resembling this man, Lord Penross."

He stopped pacing. "You seem to feel you have an idea who this man might be, Lady Charlotte."

"Yes, I do." I found this part of the story most difficult to tell. "Lord Penross, several weeks ago, I found an old newspaper—one that you had not left for me as usual in the hall. I read the account of your brother's having been sighted in Penzance. Until then, I had no idea he had been responsible for Lady Penross's death."

"Are you trying to tell me, Lady Charlotte, that the man you saw in the turret, and in Falmouth, is my brother? I find the whole idea absolutely preposterous!"

At the mention of his brother, I had seen anger rising in his face, and now it broke forth explosively.

"Do you not think I would know whether or not my brother was here in this house? Methinks your imagination must be running away with you."

"Penross is vast—I still have not explored all of its

rooms. You are away so much of the time. Is it not possible that your brother could be in hiding here? Why, the vicar told me of the priests' holes . . ."

"The vicar! Ah, yes, it is he that has put these ideas into your head."

"No, Lord Penross, it is I who have begun to piece together many incidents that have occurred since I came here."

"Perhaps you have missed your calling, Lady Charlotte. The local constabulary would be most interested in your talents," he said, turning on his heel and walking toward the door.

I had the feeling he was verbally fencing, not discussing the matter seriously. Frustrated, I pressed on, "Do I have your permission to inform them of the possible sighting in Falmouth?"

Lord Penross stopped and swung 'round. "How do you know what my brother looks like, Lady Charlotte? All portraits of him have been destroyed."

My voice shook as I said quietly, "Because there is a distinct resemblance to you, Lord Penross."

We stood looking at each other across the long, narrow, half-lit library. The tension between us was electrifying.

Despite his anger and my own misgivings, it was at that moment I knew I loved him.

17

I spent a troubled, restless night, and the next morning I breakfasted alone. Lord Penross had risen early and left for the mines; Ellie told me he had been summoned there at dawn. I prayed there would be no more trouble with the men.

As I was leaving the breakfast room, I heard a tremendous hubbub coming from the hall. Many voices seemed to be raised, and the vastness of the lofty chamber caused a resounding echo. At first I could not tell whether the mood was one of anger or pleasure, but as I turned into the hall I identified the noise as laughter, coming from a group of men whom I recognized as being miners. Their presence was greatly perturbing Rogers.

Lord Penross was in the center of the group, an expression of elation upon his face. I hung back, not wanting to intrude, but he saw me and beckoned me over to him.

"We have discovered a tin lode so vast I scarce can believe my eyes, Lady Charlotte. Your prayers have been answered!"

Seeing his joy warmed my heart. "I rejoice with you, Lord Penross. This is indeed good news."

One of the miners added heartily, "It certainly is, m' lady. What with old Boney soon to be out of the way, and now this, our families won't 'ave to worry about where their next bite o' bread'll be comin' from."

Lord Penross laughed. "There's enough to keep them in

comfort for many a year hence! I believe this calls for a service of thanksgiving, Lady Charlotte."

"The vicar has called for one for tomorrow—to thank our Lord for the great victory at Waterloo. Perhaps the services can be combined," I suggested.

"A superb idea! Men, see that your wives and children are informed of this."

I saw some of the miners look at each other knowingly, as if to say, "You won't see me or my missus in any church service." Others assured Lord Penross they would be there.

After they had left, I told Lord Penross how glad I was that the problem of the mines had now been lifted from him.

"Yes, at least one of my concerns has been resolved."

He glanced down at me before beginning to ascend the stairs. "I can only hope that there will be a solution to the . . . other problem, which has dogged me for so long."

I knew he must be referring to his brother. "I most fervently wish that, Lord Penross." I walked to the foot of the stairs—my whole being longing to reach out and touch him. "Forgive me for last night. I know you thought me most impertinent, but I still cannot get the man I saw in Falmouth out of my mind. I spent a wretched night still wondering if he were your brother."

Once more there was a flare of anger. "Put him out of your mind, Lady Charlotte. My brother has been foolhardy in the past, but not even he would dare show himself in Falmouth—or hide here within the walls of Penross."

Lord Penross turned his back and proceeded up the staircase. "Let us not think of him—let us rejoice in what God has seen fit to bring us today!"

I watched him ascend to the gallery, wishing that I could forget Justin Penross. But the fact of his presence seemed to grow more and more irrefutable in the recesses of my mind. More troubling still were my nagging doubts about Lord Penross. Had he acted as he did because he disbelieved my story—or because he knew it was true? Was Lord Penross shielding his murderous brother?

Early next morning, William and I went riding over the moors. It was chilly and somewhat brisk. A gossamer mist hung gently over the trees, and the view out to sea was interrupted by patches of low-lying clouds, foretelling showers were not far away. To the north, black smoke could now be seen trailing across the sky from the smokestacks of the mine—once more emblazoning a message of hope.

After we had been riding for about half an hour, I called to William, "It's time to go back. Your mathematics class is due to begin soon, and afterward we leave for the service of thanksgiving."

It was hard for the little boy to leave the freedom of the parkland for the confines of Miss Marsden's schoolroom. Nevertheless, he finally smiled in resignation and shouted, "We'll have to ride again this afternoon, Aunt Charlotte, if God keeps those clouds from spilling over."

I laughed as we galloped toward Penross, and felt my mood lift. The oppressive feelings that had overcome me since my visit to Falmouth were left on the moors. We tethered Guardian and the pony outside, and William and I raced each other up the steps leading to the front door.

"I won!" shouted William, forgetting to wipe his feet and receiving an instant dressing down from Rogers, who was standing in the hall.

Then the butler saw me and immediately changed his demeanor. "Oh, your ladyship, a letter arrived for you a few minutes ago." He turned to the ornate table where the post was always left and ceremoniously handed me the letter.

Excitedly, I took it from him, hoping to see Stephen's handwriting, but the script was unfamiliar. Turning over the letter I saw the seal of the War Office.

My heart sank within me. It must be news of Stephen. And in my heart I knew the news would not be good.

Rogers had left with William, and I was now alone. Sitting down on a nearby chair, I stared at the letter, but could not bring myself to open it. A numbness crept over me. I felt sure that if it were good news, I would have heard from Stephen himself. But no . . . perhaps lines of communication would be disrupted for days . . .

Finally, as if someone else was controlling my actions, I found myself tearing open the seal.

The only words I saw were—"Captain . . . Lord Stephen Winton . . . missing . . . presumed killed . . . Battle of Waterloo . . ."

The letter fell from my hands, and an agonizing cry escaped me. I stood to my feet, and for a short while reality escaped from me. Stephen . . . dead? I could not begin to comprehend it.

Without thinking what I was doing, I found myself running out of the house and down the steps, untethering Guardian, and riding along the path which followed the brink of the cliffs.

"*Presumed* killed," the letter had said.

"How dare they presume!" I shouted. The wind caught my words and swept them out to the sympathetic, turbulent sea. "How dare they . . ." Anger had taken over from shock.

I rode Guardian as fast as I could. The height of the cliffs was mesmerizing—a sheer drop to the rocks below. Yet I felt no fear for my personal safety, only an overwhelming desire to ride against the wind, away from everything and everybody. Guardian's mane lashed my face, but I was almost oblivious to it. Surely the anger, mixed with fear within me, would never subside. Dry, unrelenting sobs wracked my body as I urged the horse on.

A pathway that wound down the face of the cliff came into view, and I coaxed Guardian to venture down. I knew it led to forbidden Tregoran Cove, but I chose not to heed Lord Penross's words of warning. I cared not that ships had been wrecked there, nor that smugglers had been known to frequent the cove—I simply felt the need to ride along the bleak, deserted sands.

Reaching the end of the pathway, Guardian snorted mistrustfully at the ominous jagged rocks and patches of wet sand. He neighed, demanding we turn back, but I dug in my heels and pressed him onward. He maneuvered his way around the rotting hulls of ships that had fallen prey to wreckers in the past.

Then Guardian stumbled on something, and looking down I saw that it was a long bone, entangled in seaweed. The sea idly lapped over it, first drawing it nearer to shore, then unremittingly dragging it back again. I realized with a shock that the bone was probably human—a macabre relic from a wrecking. I shuddered and wondered to whom it had belonged. A young sailor perhaps—far from home? Had he set sail with a sense of adventure, anxious to serve his country? The willful sea, an accomplice in his death, was impersonally now his grave.

Anger now swelled inside of me, overpowering the numbness. "Is this how my brother will be found, God? Just a skeleton strewn on a cold, unfeeling, foreign battlefield?" I threw my head back, and at the top of my lungs, cried above the sound of the surf, "Don't You care? Don't You care about the ones You've created?"

I rode on, out of the forbidding cove. Hostile rage was still my companion—tearing into me, not letting its hold slacken.

"Stephen was all I had, Father . . ."

My own words made me rein in Guardian, and I slumped over the saddle—as the tears flowed down my cheeks.

"Is he dead? Oh, God, You know."

I looked out toward the horizon. The world seemed emptier. The joy Stephen and I had known as children, and continued to have as we grew up together, would be gone forever—snuffed out on a battlefield. All because of an egomaniac dictator with an insatiable ambition.

I felt hollow, unreal. The loneliness of the beach echoed my feeling of isolation.

John Wesley's words came back to me: "The believer . . . feels the love of God shed abroad in his heart. It is the internal evidence of Christianity . . ."

But I felt *nothing*—nothing but rage and pain. "I do not sense Your love, oh God. Do You demand more of me? Is my faith nothing to You, or must You exact more from this bewildered believer?"

I rode on and on, not caring in which direction, thinking of all I had ever hoped for from life. Now it seemed I had joined the ranks of those who, from ships out to sea, had seen the lamps of the wreckers that promised safe harbor. Reality had dawned when they were dashed upon the merciless rocks.

The light of hope promised by the Church had lured me on to a supposed belief that God answers prayer—that somehow I could have a part in seeing those I loved kept safe and secure. And my hopes, too, had been dashed on the rocks of despair. (The fact that the Church—unlike the wreckers—did not deliberately delude did not lessen the cruel outcome in my eyes.)

A bitterness such as I had never experienced before now cloaked me. The leaden skies were in keeping with my mood. Soon stinging rain began to fall.

The tide was beginning to come in, and I had ridden several miles from Penross. The thought of being trapped in Tregoran Cove urged me to turn Guardian around and head back in the direction of the manor.

The proud, Elizabethan house dominated the coast-line—even from miles away. In the distance I could make out the chapel roof, and I thought of Lady Penross's murder. It was no wonder that Lord Penross had been bitter toward the Church. I began to understand his feelings; shallow platitudes did not satisfy the angry questions that now besieged me. If my faith had faltered after my parents' deaths, it was now in peril of dying out altogether.

Guardian seemed to sense danger as we returned to Tregoran Cove. His pace slackened, and I had to bend down and coax him on. Then, without any warning, he stumbled, and I was thrown.

The impact sent pain wracking through my body. For several moments I lay there, stunned. Then I rolled over to see that Guardian was trapped in a patch of wet sand—his eyes ablaze with fear. Instantly, I remembered that Cornwall was infamous for patches of quicksand that could fatally envelop unwary people—and animals! That had been another reason Lord Penross had forbidden the children to go to the seaside.

Forgetting my own pain, I managed to get on my feet. Grabbing the reins, I tried to urge Guardian out of the mire. He freed his forelegs, then reared up, causing his hind legs to sink even deeper, and his frantic plunging only worsened the situation. I started to panic as I thought of being trapped in the grip of this frightening cove—the incoming tide fast advancing—but Guardian's cries reminded me I must remain calm. Murmuring reassuring words, I knelt, and somehow persuaded him to roll over on his side. From there, gradually, with my encouragement, he was able to inch his way out of the treacherous patch of sand. Finally, he stood and shook himself, his eyes still wild with fear, but trusting me. I gently soothed him, brushing the sand from his lathered coat, and led him away from the danger and grim reminders of the past.

As we walked back through the cove, I became aware of a small boat anchored near the mouth of a narrow inlet which led to a cave. No doubt the boat had been there earlier; in my grief and anger I had failed to notice it. Then I remembered seeing it there when I first looked down on the forbidding cove—two men had watched me, then disappeared behind the rocks. I shivered at the memory and hurriedly urged Guardian through the cove and up the winding path around the cliff. I was thankful he had not been hurt and anxious to be away from the frightening, jagged rocks which loomed round me like gigantic hostile sentinels.

I was aching from my fall, and the rain was pelting down, but I decided to walk Guardian back to Penross; he was lathered and still disturbed. My concern for him had brought me back to the immediate world—a world I now had to face.

I saw that the horse was bedded down, then climbed the steps to the manor, thankful there was no one in the hall. I was soaked to the skin and the rain and wind had wreaked havoc with my hair. Sand was still embedded in my riding habit, and my eyes were swollen from crying. I needed to repair to my room and be alone with my grief.

I had taken only a few steps, however, when Mrs. Dawson, the housekeeper, appeared.

"Mercy, yer ladyship—whatever 'as 'appened to ye?" Her usual hostility toward me vanished, and she hovered over me, not knowing quite what to do.

"I am perfectly all right, Mrs. Dawson. I merely had a fall from Guardian. Some hot water and quiet are all I need at present."

I walked past her, avoiding her gaze.

"But Lord Penross and the children are awaiting ye at the church, m'lady. 'Ave you forgotten the service of thanksgiving?"

I halted—my whole being rebelling at the thought of attending such a service. For there was no room for thanksgiving in my heart; it was too full of anger and bitter resentment . . .

"I shall not be joining them, Mrs. Dawson." And I left her with her mouth gaping in astonishment as I stiffly climbed the stairs.

18

The rain beating against the windowpane awakened me before dawn. Apparently, it had rained all night.

I had finally fallen asleep from sheer exhaustion, having given instructions that I was not to be disturbed. There had been several taps upon my door, but I had refused to answer them—not wanting to face anyone. My belligerent, bitter mood had now waned, leaving me unsure and remorseful. I had never experienced such harsh, violent feelings before, and guilt now became allied with grief and doubt. Emotionally, I was spent.

Stephen stared at me from the miniature by my bed.

"Is this all that is left—someone else's impression of you?" I pushed back the sheets and, getting out of bed, took the small painting of my brother over to the window seat. I propped it next to the toy soldiers that had been his as a child, the ones William had left to "guard" me against Napoleon.

Sitting down, I curled my feet up under me and picked up one of the soldiers. He was dressed in a bright red jacket and holding a saber aloft in his right hand; he stared heroically into the distance. His jet-black steed looked equally noble, head bowed and left foreleg raised.

"When you played with these soldiers, Stephen, did you imagine that this is what war would be like? Exciting, heroic, and when you tired of it the game could be put away for another day?"

I must have sat holding the toy soldier and thinking of Stephen for over an hour.

My thoughts were interrupted by the sound of something being pushed under my door. Still aching from my fall from Guardian, I walked over to the door and picked up the papers lying there. They were from William and Elizabeth. A short letter, signed by both of them, expressed their sorrow at my news—"But don't give up hope, Aunt Charlotte, we are praying and we love you."

I was deeply touched by their thoughtfulness—and especially by the fact that it was from both of them. William could always be counted on to encourage me, but for Elizabeth to include herself greatly heartened me.

They had also painted two scenes for me. William's was of his pony jumping one of the ha-ha ditches, and Elizabeth had depicted a delicate bouquet of flowers. I propped up the two paintings on either side of the clock on the mantlepiece and smiled in spite of myself.

It was then that I caught sight of my reflection in the mirror. Dark, hollow eyes stared back at me. I could not let the children see me looking this way. Somehow I would have to pull myself together before I could venture out of my room.

Ellie's familiar knock on the door—exactly on time as always with my hot water—made me realize that the clockwork schedule of the house would keep on running, whether I felt like it or not. She swept into the room, carrying a breakfast tray—followed by a chambermaid encumbered with a steaming kettle of hot water. Ellie ordered her to stand it by the washstand and then leave.

"I really don't feel hungry, Ellie," I protested, looking down at the tray laden with toast, two silver-covered dishes, and tea.

"Beggin' yer pardon, m'lady, I 'ad strict instructions from Lord Penross before 'e left that you was to eat well. And 'ere—there's a note and a book from 'im. I know you don't feel like talking about it, but I want you to know that we're all worried about you, and 'oping that you get good news soon . . ."

Ellie was unable to look me in the face the whole time she was speaking, and when she was finished, she quickly made her way out of the bedchamber. I was left looking down at Lord Penross's note, propped up in the toast rack. I saw that the book was his copy of William Blake's verse. I read his note before opening the book:

Dear Lady Charlotte,
Forgive me for reading the letter from the War Office. I found it in the hall. Needless to say, I share your concern and trust you will hear all is well.
I regret having to leave at this time, but expect to return in four days.
I am not one who is easily able to express my feelings at times like these. I leave Blake to declare them for me . . ."

I folded his note and, still keeping it in my hand, I reached for the book of poems. My letter from the War Office was partly visible; I opened the book to see that Lord Penross had used it as a bookmark. He had underlined some of the lines from the poem entitled, "On Another's Sorrow":

> Can I see another's woe,
> And not be in sorrow too?
> Can I see another's grief,
> And not seek for kind relief?
>
> Can I see a falling tear,
> And not feel my sorrow's share? . . .

Gradually I began to respond to Lord Penross's sensitivity, and the simple, comforting words of the poet. I read on:

> He doth give his joy to all;
> He becomes an infant small;
> He becomes a man of woe;
> He doth feel the sorrow too.
>
> Think not thou canst sigh a sigh
> And thy maker is not by;
> Think not thou canst weep a tear
> And thy maker is not near.

Oh! he gives to us his joy
That our grief he may destroy . . .

I replaced the letter from the War Office within the pages
of Blake's poems. Clasping the book and Lord Penross's
letter to me, I slowly walked to the window and looked out
at the rain-sodden grounds. I remembered something my
mother had said, so many years before, about God's love:

"Perhaps the greatest assurance we can have of His caring is in the kindnesses He places within another's heart
for us. These are tangible evidences of His love . . ."

I looked across at the two paintings the children had
done for me and their note. Then, looking down at their
father's expression of kindness in my hands, I began to
read Blake's poem again:

Can I see another's woe . . .

I allowed myself the indulgence of tears, for they were
now tears of thanksgiving—and hope—as well as pain.

The rain did not cease for three days. Being confined to
the house greatly added to my feelings of helplessness as I
waited anxiously for further communication concerning
Stephen. I also found myself missing Lord Penross acutely.
His sharing of Blake's poem had made me even more aware
of the sensitivity he so often disguised with a brusque
manner, and I longed to express my true feelings to him. I
carried his book of Blake's poetry wherever I went and
restlessly awaited the day of his return.

When the newspaper was delivered from London, I anxiously scanned the columns devoted to the account of the
Battle of Waterloo. I learned that the Coldstream Guards
and the Scots Guards had been responsible for defending the
main gate of Hougoumont Chateau, upon which the whole
outcome of the conflict depended. The Duke of Wellington
conceded that without their valiant and sacrificial effort,
the battle would have been lost.

There had been many casualties. I could hardly bring
myself to read about them.

After the battle had been won, forty thousand men and

ten thousand horses had been found dead or dying. Some of the wounded men had been taken to farmhouses and cottages in the area . . .

I read this last bit of news over and over again, pinning all my hopes of Stephen's survival upon it. Perhaps even now he was recovering in an isolated farmhouse . . . Oh, how I prayed this was so.

The vicar called, but I had given instructions not to be disturbed; I felt too embarrassed by my outburst of anger toward God to see him. He left a note expressing his concern and telling me that my brother and I were constantly in his prayers. "May grief not be your constant companion, but hope, which can transcend your fears . . ."

In a postscript to his note he added: "Concerning the other matter—I have been unable to gather any information." For a moment I did not understand what he meant, and then I remembered our conversation in the sunken gardens and the vicar's promise to do what he could to find out the latest news about Justin Penross's whereabouts.

In my anxiety over Stephen, I had almost forgotten that other source of my worry. But the vicar's note caused me to ponder anew. Perhaps my surmise that I had seen the Honorable Justin at Falmouth was, after all, incorrect. These past days had brought no new evidence that he was in the house. But then I had been so preoccupied, hardly leaving my room except to teach the children.

I felt in need of exercise—it seemed as if the rain would never stop—so I decided to walk up and down the gallery. Noiselessly I opened the door and looked out—no one was in sight. The great house felt damp and uninviting, and I almost turned back, but I could not remain within the confines of my room any longer.

Listening for a moment at the nursery door, I could hear Miss Marsden's voice droning on as she taught the children. William must be itching to be outside, too. I looked forward to spending time with the children later in the day.

The long gallery was almost in darkness, even though it was scarcely two o'clock. How I detested this weather that added an aura of gloom to everything! I tried to offset this sense of melancholy by trying to imagine Penross Manor years before, when the east wing, including the sinister

Green Room, would have been occupied. The gallery would have been filled with people promenading up and down, discussing the events of those days. Perhaps music could have been heard filtering up to the lofty rotunda in the hall, and laughter would have echoed throughout the great house.

As I walked along the gallery toward the east wing, I noticed a door slightly ajar and saw that it led to the north wing of the house. The door had always been closed before, and Ellie had told me it led to the part of the manor that had not been used for many years—"Long before Lord Penross was born, your ladyship."

Bored with the dismal gallery, I decided to explore, and hesitantly pushed open the door. Immediately I found myself in a corridor which overlooked the same overgrown courtyard I had seen the first day I visited the family chapel.

The corridor's tall windows were darkened with years of grime, and in the gloomy half-light the abandoned wing of the house took on an eerie atmosphere. I turned back, but then noticed that a door to one of the rooms was open. I looked inside and saw a bedchamber, which had once been magnificent but now was covered in cobwebs—the bed hangings rotting on the elegant four-poster bed. Damask curtains, framing the sullen windows, had met with the same fate, and threadbare chairs and a love seat stood forlornly abandoned in the middle of the chamber.

I quickly left and walked on down the corridor, glancing in at several other chambers—all in the same state of deterioration. At one time they must have been for guests —all exquisitely furnished with the finest acquisitions from London and Europe. But the ravages of time and neglect had wrought their havoc.

An oppressive sadness engulfed me, and I left the last deserted room feeling more than ever the need for fresh air. The atmosphere was stifling.

Further down the hall I saw another door, half open. It seemed different from the rest; the dark oak, linen-fold paneling had an even more dismal air. I pushed the door open and peered inside.

Tiers of discarded furniture were precariously stacked

up to the ceiling almost blocking the little light that managed to come through the filthy windows. Worm-eaten beams looked as if they would disintegrate should the mass of cobwebs that hung from them be disturbed. I stood there aghast at the sight of such decay.

A feeling of apprehension came over me, and I turned to leave. It was then that I saw, propped up in the far righthand corner of the appalling room, something that made my blood run cold.

A portrait of a man was staring at me. His eyes seemed to follow me—eyes I had seen before. I gasped and put my hands to my lips. The face staring at me from the canvas was clearly the face I had seen at the turret window and at Falmouth.

It had to be Justin Penross! His face bore the Penross characteristics, but his eyes—although dark like Lord Penross's—were cold and calculating. The sneer that curled his mouth gave him an evil expression.

Lord Penross had said that all portraits of his brother had been destroyed. Then why had this one been saved? I noted that the portrait, unlike the rest of the room, was free of dust . . .

It was then that I thought I heard footsteps coming down the corridor toward the room. I listened intently, at first thinking it was my imagination. But, no, the steps were coming nearer and nearer. Hastily I looked around for a place to hide, but there was only time to slip behind the open door.

The footsteps stopped outside the room, and whoever it was hesitated before entering. Then I heard the person walk over to the corner where the portrait stood.

My heart was beating so loudly, I was certain whoever it was could hear it . . .

Through a crack in the door, I was able to make out a figure. I could only see that it was a woman, and that she was bending over the portrait. She pulled out from her sleeve a handkerchief and began dusting the painting.

Afterwards, the woman stood for a few more minutes gazing down at the portrait, then left the room. As she did so, she closed the door with a resounding slam, and I was left alone in that dark, decaying room—my hands behind me, pressing against the wall, my heart pounding in terror that I had been locked in.

The Honorable Justin Penross's eyes mocked at me through the half-light. My spine felt as if an icy hand had been placed upon it, and it was all that I could do not to run and open the door.

It seemed an eternity before the sound of the woman's footsteps could be heard no more. With trembling hands I opened the door and fled the deserted hall.

19

*L*ater *that afternoon, William stood at my door, his toy* Noah's ark tucked under his arm.

"Aunt Charlotte, may I bring this to play with, while you read to us? If it rains any more we may need to build one of these . . ." His pretense of solemnity was belied by the twinkle in his eye.

He ran into the room, followed by Elizabeth, who was shaking her head at him.

"How could we ever build one in time, William? Besides, Penross is built on a granite cliff, and I doubt whether the water would rise as high as that." Elizabeth was in a doleful mood and refused to be drawn into any more of our conversation. She concentrated on her petit point.

Undeterred, William spread out all the carved wooden animals on the oriental rug in front of the fireplace and proceeded to march them all in and out of the ark.

I had told the children that since we could not go outside before tea, I would read them a story. William had insisted that this would not be in place of my reading to him *after* tea—or would it? I had reassured him with a smile. Now, watching him line up each animal with a look of determination, I could not help but reach out and touch the top of his blond, curly head.

Having the children with me helped somewhat to dispel

the aching void that had become part of me since hearing that Stephen was missing.

Elizabeth came by my chair and asked me to help her with a difficulty she had encountered with her embroidery. I marveled once more in the change in her manner toward me. Since our day in Falmouth, she seemed to have completely accepted me, although there was still a measure of reserve in our relationship. I longed to be able to show her affection, but felt it was still too early for her to accept.

When the maid brought tea to us a little later, Miss Marsden followed her in. I had invited the governess to take tea with us. In the past weeks—perhaps feeling a need to reestablish her influence with Elizabeth—Miss Marsden had surprised me by accepting several of my invitations to join me and the children, although she never relaxed her accustomed air of stern disapproval. Even now, as she stood in the doorway, her first words were an admonishment to William to put all his animals away—"At once!" Just by her presence—poor woman—Miss Marsden had the gift of making any room feel twenty degrees cooler.

It was while she was stirring the sugar in her tea that I noticed something which made me pause in a conversation I was having with William. Protruding from the cuff of her left sleeve was a lace-bordered handkerchief. It was extremely dirty, and out of keeping with her normally well-scrubbed, immaculate appearance.

I looked at her intently as she bent over Elizabeth's embroidery, pointing out the flaws. I half shut my eyes and tried to imagine whether or not it was Miss Marsden I had seen dusting the portrait in that dark, frightening room only an hour or so ago.

"Aunt Charlotte, the expression on your face is so funny," laughed William. "Is something wrong with your eyes?"

"Oh, no, William." I looked away from Miss Marsden as she turned to see what was the matter. "Please hand me Miss Marsden's cup. I am sure she would like me to replenish it with more tea."

"I have had sufficient, thank you, Lady Charlotte. Now, if you will excuse me, I have to leave. I would ask you to please remain observant of the children's bedtime." She rose, and as she walked to the door, I was positive that it was Miss Marsden I had seen dusting Justin Penross's portrait.

I would speak of this to Lord Penross when he returned.

The rain finally stopped, and the wonderful silence, as I lay in my bed that night, was most welcome. Tomorrow, we would be able to ride again. A full moon shone through the tattered remaining clouds to light up my bedchamber. The only sound to be heard was that of the sea in the distance, almost lulling me to sleep. But thoughts of Stephen kept coming back to me.

"Oh, God, I pray that he is safe this night . . ."

I wished that I were a man, so that I could go to Belgium and try and find him myself. Perhaps I would go at any rate! When Lord Penross returned, I would ask him if there were any way I could make the journey. Perhaps I could persuade my aunt to travel with me.

Lady Sanford had written me a strange letter this week, commiserating about Stephen, then saying that she had been to my house in London. "Such a difference—but then, perhaps, I should not be saying this . . ."

What difference? Did she mean that it was in such disrepair? I had written to my servant, dear Jenkins, asking him to see that everything was well taken care of. But I knew he was elderly and not capable of taking on alone the responsibility of such a large house. I only wished I could employ someone to help him, but my resources were so sparse . . ."

I tossed and turned, and found that sleep evaded me.

The sound of someone in the corridor, and then a door opening, caused me to sit up in bed. I looked over to make sure that I had securely bolted mine. Then I listened, but could hear nothing. Perhaps one of the children needed something. I got out of bed and, noiselessly drawing back the bolt, opened the door a fraction.

The door to the nursery was shut. I peered down the gallery, and saw that Lord Penross's door was open. He must have returned! In the darkness, I could just make out the figure of a man coming out of the room—then he turned and looked back in again. He stood there for some time, gazing toward the wall where I knew Lady Penross's portrait hung.

Finally, he stepped back into the moonlight. From the painting I had seen in the north wing, I recognized him as Justin Penross—and the expression on his handsome face was one of bitter longing. He then closed the door and began to walk down the gallery, past the suits of armor in the east wing . . . toward the Green Room.

I shut my door and bolted it. I was shaking almost uncontrollably.

How could I inform the constabulary of Justin's presence here? I went over to ring for Ellie, then realized she had gone to her mother's for the weekend and would not be home until tomorrow.

I had assured her it would be perfectly all right. Now I wished I had not been so accommodating.

I realized how chilled I was, and reached for my dressing gown. Far out to sea I could see William's "glowworms"— the fishing fleet lights twinkled and danced on the water, adding to the beauty of the moonlight. But I noticed their beauty only peripherally; my thoughts were still with Justin, wondering why he would risk his sanctuary just to gaze into Lord Penross's chamber. Was it Lady Caroline's portrait that drew him?

I looked down at the sunken gardens, gazing at the statuary bathed in light. I was about to go back to bed—there was nothing I could do about Justin tonight—when I thought I saw something move behind the privet hedges of the maze.

There it was again!

This time I saw that it was the top of a man's hat. Then, under a large oak tree, I could dimly make out the forms of two men standing in the shadows. One beckoned to the man in the maze, and he stealthily ran to them.

I could not make out their faces, but they were deep in conversation, and I saw them point to the house, then to the west—in the direction of Tregoran Cove. One man continued to stare up at the house, and I stepped back out of the moonlight, fearing he would see me. When I looked down again, I saw one of the men signaling with his hands toward the east wing.

They must be signaling to Justin.

In an instant the men disappeared into the woods which led down to the sea. I sat watching, in case Justin followed them, but after some time I crawled back into bed and sat there listening, waiting . . .

I must have fallen asleep, for I was awakened by a sound I had heard before one other moonlit night—the low, grinding sound of a wagon or some other heavily laden conveyance.

I ran over to the window that looked out to the west, and to Tregoran Cove, and I could see lights, and a large ship with great sails, way out to sea.

Surely they were not trying to wreck the ship!

But then I remembered that wrecking only took place on dark, stormy nights, when sailors could be lured into thinking the cove was a safe harbor.

They must be smugglers—and the men I had seen earlier were part of the operation.

I watched at the window but could not see what was going on in the cove. I was convinced Justin must be involved in some way . . .

A movement from beneath a tree, just across from my window caught my eye. I looked down into the shadows, and could barely make out the figure of a man. Had he seen me as I surveyed what was going on at the cove? Surely not!

He doffed his hat and bowed to the waist. I stepped back from the window, not knowing whether it was Justin or one of the men I had seen signaling to the house.

Terrified, I ran from the window, and clutched one of the bedposts—conscious of the fact that there was nowhere in the vast house that I could go for help.

20

At regular intervals during the night, I heard the low rumbling of wagons, and I prayed that the King's preventive men would sight the smuggler's ship and catch the men red-handed. Surely from some vantage point along the coast they would have seen the lights as the men signaled to the ship.

What kept me relatively calm was the knowledge that Lord Penross was returning today. I kept this uppermost in my mind, for I was filled with apprehension. Justin was beginning to flaunt his presence. His visit to Lord Penross's chambers had made me fear he was planning, in some way, to cause Lord Penross harm.

Over and over again I thought that I should send someone to alert the constabulary. But who? I had no way of being sure who in the household was aware of the smuggling. I also remembered how angry Lord Penross had been when I had told him I believed Justin was in the house and had suggested informing the law. I felt it best to tarry until Lord Penross returned.

When morning arrived, I waited impatiently for Ellie to bring hot water—then remembered once more that she had gone to be with her mother. I rang the bell, and finally a frightened chambermaid arrived.

"Sorry m'lady, everythin's late this mornin'. Cook couldn't get the fire to light . . . and Mrs. Dawson's not well. Neither's 'er son Tom . . ."

"I quite understand. When it is convenient, would you see that hot water is brought to me as soon as is possible?"

She nodded, and gave a quick curtsy, then ran from the room. The poor girl was genuinely distressed, and I wondered what had been going on in the kitchen to frighten her. Or did she know what had transpired last night?

About an hour later the hot water finally arrived, and I was able to dress. I had little appetite, but thought that I would need all my strength to cope with the day ahead of me, so I decided to eat a light breakfast. Quickly walking along the gallery to the top of the stairs, I felt as if at any moment Justin would appear.

The breakfast room was bright and sunny, and I sat at the table in the window looking out over the parkland. It was a beautiful morning, with a sky of brilliant blue—a perfect day for riding. But the thought of Justin and the men I had seen last night caused me to reconsider.

Breakfast was sparse indeed, and I was glad my appetite was small. The toast was decidedly burnt, and the dish of porridge cold and lumpy. It was obvious that the kitchen was in disarray, and Rogers came to apologize to me personally.

I watched his eyes as he was explaining the reason for the inconvenience. "The wretched chimney, m'lady. The rain has caused some damage, which I trust we will be able to rectify shortly."

The steely eyes showed no hint of awareness that anything untoward was going on—but then his expression was always difficult to read.

"I am sorry to hear Mrs. Dawson is unwell, Rogers."

He hesitated for a moment. "Oh, I'm sure it is nothing serious, m'lady. She should be fine soon. Whatever it is seems to have smitten Tom, the footman, too."

He straightened the tablecloth and, avoiding my gaze, picked up a solitary crumb. There was something different about his demeanor today—something I could not fathom.

"Has the newspaper arrived from London this morning, Rogers?"

"No, m'lady. Everything has been delayed. The storms have affected most of the southland. I would hazard a guess that Lord Penross may have been detained. I hear that the streets in Exeter were like turbulent rivers for several days."

My heart sank within me, for I had been counting the hours until his return.

"I trust he will soon be safely home, Rogers."

"Oh, yes, m'lady—we all do."

I thought I detected a note of cynicism in his voice, but could not be certain. Rogers left the breakfast room, and I drank my last sip of tea, contemplating the terrible journey that Lord Penross may have experienced. I reached for my serviette and was about to wipe the corners of my mouth when the door burst open. There stood Elizabeth, her eyes wide with fear.

"William is missing! No one has seen him this morning!"

I jumped up from my chair and ran to her. "What are you saying? Have you not seen him in the nursery? Did you have breakfast with him?"

"No. Everything was so late this morning. I stayed in bed until the nurserymaid brought up a tray. Miss Marsden hasn't seen him either. When she went in to awaken him, his bed was empty . . ."

I tried to control the dread that now assailed me. "Perhaps he awakened early and went out for a walk; you know how he has been counting the hours until the rain stopped."

She shook her head, growing more frantic. "His pony is missing, too. William's more than likely fallen somewhere. You always encouraged him too much about riding. Miss Marsden thinks so, too . . ."

"I cannot believe William would have been so disobedient. He knows he is not allowed to ride on his own."

Elizabeth ran from the room, tears streaming down her face. I started to go after her, but decided instead to instruct Rogers to see that Guardian was immediately brought round to the front door. I ran to my room and changed into my riding habit. If William were out riding on his own, then perhaps I knew where he had gone.

As I was about to mount Guardian, Rogers appeared at the door. "Your ladyship, William's pony has been found, near the approach to the moors, wandering by one of the ha-ha ditches. . . ."

I did not wait to answer him but rode off at full speed

toward the moors. William must be lying somewhere—injured.

"Dear Lord, please help me find this child . . ."

I followed the ditches around the whole perimeter of the estate, but could not see any trace of William. The gulls swooped mournfully over the parkland, adding to my mood of depression and mounting concern. I decided to follow the boundary again, but there was still no sign of him.

I kept calling his name over and over, but all I could hear was the sound of the gulls, and in the distance the church bells chiming the hour. I counted to twelve, and could not believe I had been looking for him nearly three hours.

Before I went back to the manor, I took the path which led past Tregoran Cove, still calling William as loudly as I could. I stopped Guardian and looked down into the cove, although the horse snorted and danced skittishly, anxious to be away from the place. The tide was now in, covering any evidence of last night's smuggling. The small boat, however, was still anchored by the mouth of the cave. Had they used it to transport their contraband from the big ship?

I could not spend any more time contemplating what might have taken place—William had to be found. My heart ached for the little boy. I had such a love for this child; the thought of his coming to harm was almost too much to endure.

I rode back to Penross Manor, hoping there might be good news—that someone else had found him and brought him home. Tethering Guardian, I ran into the hall, calling for Rogers or Mrs. Dawson. No one came, and the house was deathly quiet. I raced up the stairs, hopeful that I would find William in the nursery, but it was empty.

Feeling defeated and desperately afraid, I went to my room. The door was wide open, and the first thing I saw—lying on the parquet floor—was the yellow Easter dress I had had made for Elizabeth. The pretty bonnet lay crushed and torn beside the dress, its ribbons dirty and bedraggled. It looked as if it had been stamped upon . . .

I picked it up and futilely tried to straighten the brim. It seemed that my hard-won friendship with Elizabeth was as broken as the delicate yellow bonnet I held in my hands.

"Oh, God, please—please help me find William. And let Elizabeth know how much I love her . . ."

I was interrupted by the swish of a skirt. Turning, I saw Miss Marsden standing in the doorway, Elizabeth at her side.

"I see you have not found William. I prophesied no good would come of your encouraging him to ride so far from the house." Miss Marsden looked smug and condescending. "What a welcome for Lord Penross when he returns to find his son is lost, your ladyship."

Elizabeth came over to me, and snatched the bonnet from my hand—throwing it into the fireplace. "I hate you! We didn't need you, or your gifts. I wish you'd never come here!"

She ran into the nursery, and before Miss Marsden joined her, I saw a look of triumph in the austere governess's eyes.

I felt as if a knife had penetrated my heart, but I held back the tears. There was no time for self-pity. I had to find William.

Rogers was in the hall, and I gave him instructions to send someone for the constable. "Tell him to come here immediately, Rogers. We have to find William before dark. I am going out again to search."

"That has already been taken care of, m'lady." He started to leave, then turned back. "Oh, I forgot to tell you—Lord Penross has been delayed. A messenger brought the news a short time ago. However, he expects to return to Penross this evening."

I clenched my hands in an effort to control myself. Now more than ever I needed Lord Penross's strength.

"Well, Rogers, please do all you can, and ask the other servants to keep searching for William, too. Any small clue could be the means for finding him . . ."

I left Penross feeling completely dejected, but for the sake of the child I had to keep on searching. This time I went down to where we had often sat and painted. The dell surrounded by trees was deserted. Dismounting, I scrutinized the ground to see whether there was any sign that William might have been there this morning. He often surprised me with small sketches.

The remembrance of the painting of his pony and the ha-ha ditch brought tears to my eyes.

Holding Guardian's reins, I looked out to sea.

"Is it useless to pray for William, God?"

A feeling of bitterness came over me again. Were all my pleas to Him to no avail? It was as if I were in a wilderness, and I had never felt so alone.

Mounting, I turned the horse toward Penross once more.

21

Guardian was exhausted and in need of water. I rode to the stables to find them deserted—Harris nowhere to be seen. I thought he must still be out searching for William, whose piebald pony was standing forlornly in its stall. I filled two buckets with water from the pump and gave them to the pony and Guardian, then fed them both some oats. Before leaving, the pony nuzzled my hand, sensing something was wrong. I patted him, whispering, "I'm sure you know what has happened to William. If only you could speak . . ."

I led Guardian back to the manor, and tethered him there, knowing I might have to ride out again. I felt weary, defeated. The sky was beginning to cloud over, and I knew it would not be long before dusk. The thought of William being lost all night urged me on.

I was hungry, yet taking time to eat was out of the question. Passing the dining room, I looked in, and saw that the table was not laid. I rang the bell, hoping that someone would answer and I could obtain at least tea or cocoa to revive me. Minutes went by, and the only sound in the room was the ticking of the grandfather clock. No one answered my ring.

A large, crystal and silver epergne stood in the center of the table, and fortunately it was filled with fruit. I gathered some grapes, apples, and pears—thinking that I could eat these as I continued my search. From the sideboard I took a bowl and filled it with the fruit. Also on the sideboard was a large covered cheese dish, and I cut a wedge of cheddar, adding it to the fruit. The bread that had been left out was stale to the touch; nevertheless, I took some slices. A large ewer contained drinking water, and I poured myself a glass.

It was while I was quenching my thirst that I thought I heard a sound coming from the minstrel gallery at the north end of the great room. I looked up to see something move in the darkness, but could not make out what it was. The same asphyxiating sensation came over me that I had experienced in the chapel when I had felt someone was there. I picked up the bowl of fruit and fled from the room.

Stopping in the hall only long enough to ring the bell for Rogers, I ran up the staircase and along to the gallery. The nursery door was open, and I looked in to see Miss Marsden's door shut, but Elizabeth's ajar. I knocked and looked in to see Elizabeth sitting at the window, shoulders slumped in dejection.

I whispered, "Have you heard any news of William?"

She shook her head, and did not look round at me.

Walking over to her, I placed my hand on her shoulder and felt her body tense. "Elizabeth, I know you are angry with me at present, but please, please, listen to me and obey what I have to say. Lock your door, and do not open it under any circumstances until I come back."

I took several pieces of fruit from the bowl, along with some of the cheese and bread, and laid them on a dish. "Elizabeth, eat this, and please remember, do not leave your room, no matter who asks you to—not even Miss Marsden. Lock the door behind me. I am afraid something is terribly wrong, and I am going to try and get help. Have you seen the constable?"

Elizabeth turned to look at me and shook her head; her eyes were swollen from crying. I left the room and quietly shut the door. A few seconds later, I heard the key turn and the bolt slide into place.

I looked over to the shut door of Miss Marsden's room and tiptoed past it—not wanting to encounter her. I was more and more convinced I could trust nobody in this house.

Once in my room, I rang and rang and rang the bell—no one came. My fears were beginning to be realized—there were no servants in the house. Were Mrs. Dawson and Tom really ill, or had they, too, joined in some kind of conspiracy? I thought of visiting their rooms, but the servants' quarters were accessible only by venturing down a long, dark corridor.

The certainty that Justin was prowling throughout the manor terrified me. And I had come to the frightening realization that Rogers had perhaps not sent for the constabulary.

It was now dark, and the moon was intermittently shining through the clouds. I prayed that I would soon hear Lord Penross's coach. But I could not wait for his arrival. Pacing up and down my room, I tried to put into perspective what I should do next.

Invoking the vicar's assistance was the only answer. I felt uncomfortable doing so—I had rejected his consolation after I had heard news of Stephen, and I still felt shame over my angry outburst toward God. But I must put aside my pride and doubts; there was no other person to whom I could go for help.

I looked down at Lord Penross's book lying on my bedside table, and remembered Blake's words of consolation:

> Think not thou canst sigh a sigh
> And thy maker is not by . . .

John Wesley's words also echoed in my mind: "The believer . . . feels the love of God . . ."

And I whispered through my wall of disillusionment, "God, be with me this night, I pray. I need Your love as never before . . ."

I hastily ate a portion of the fruit and cheese and left my room, walking stealthily along the gallery to the staircase. Only the thought of trying to help William kept me going— every shadow seemed to hold the presence of Justin Penross.

In the patchy moonlight, the stairs and great hall appeared vaster than ever before, and I ran across the white marble floor, past the statues and formidable portraits, and flung open the front door, thankful to be outside.

Guardian was nowhere to be seen.

I knew that I had securely tied him. Frantically, I called his name, and I ran up and down the gravel driveway outside the house, trying to see if he had wandered off. There was no sign of him. The thought that Harris had taken him back to the stables crossed my mind, but I feared if I went there I would encounter Justin.

I looked back at the forbidding house—it was all in darkness. I knew I could not go back inside. I had to get help.

Tearing a white silk scarf from my neck, I bound it around the outer and inner latch of the front door. If Lord Penross or Ellie should return, they would know I must have left in haste and would not lock me out. I had no such trust in the rest of the household, but I had no choice but to leave.

I stood for a moment contemplating the long walk in semidarkness to the vicarage. The shortcut through the woods would save a great deal of time, but I was fearful indeed of having to walk through the graveyard—it had seemed ominous even when I rode through it in broad daylight. I had laughed at Tom when he spoke of ghosts in the graveyard. But it was not the thought of ghosts that frightened me now—it was Justin and the men who were in collusion with him. Nevertheless, I ran down the driveway and into the woods, with my compelling concern for William and Elizabeth giving me the resolution to go on.

The woods were muddy from the heavy rains, and I found it hard to walk along the uneven pathway. Overgrowing branches and briars kept tearing at my face and clothes. At first, the eerie stillness was frightening, and each time I paused I kept listening, expecting to hear footsteps following me. I turned several times, convinced that someone was there. The snap of a twig, the rustle of leaves, the murmur of a breeze from the sea—all added to my apprehension that I was not the only one traversing these misty, shadowed woods.

I came to the gate which led to the graveyard and lifted the latch, my heart beating wildly. But in the distance I could see a light upstairs in the vicarage. Thank God someone was home; help would not be far off now . . .

The path that led through the graveyard was now especially dark and menacing. Not even a glimmer of moonlight infiltrated the somber mass of vines, which had grown into a tunnel-like archway along the path. The alternative was to go several minutes out of my way. I chose the graveyard path, praying as I went that no one would be lurking in the shadows. The somber, gray gravestones, with their mounds of green grass, seemed like silent witnesses to my desperate mission.

With all the strength I could muster, I ran along the shrouded path, pushing away the vines that hung like clinging tentacles in the darkness. I felt as if I would never come to the end of the suffocating tunnel. I dared not look back, but kept staring ahead of me, to the solitary light in the vicarage. As I emerged from the vines, an owl, which must have been perched atop them, gave a sudden screech and flew in front of me, swooping down to snatch up a fieldmouse who had had the misfortune to venture forth.

Out of breath, I hurried along by the walls of the somber granite church, looking neither to the left or right, until I reached the vicarage and stumbled through the overgrown garden. Finally, I clasped the iron ring and pulled the bell, leaning against the wall and shaking from fear and exhaustion.

No one answered.

I rang again.

"Dear God, let someone be at home!"

A casement window above me slowly opened, and the nightcapped, bespectacled face of the vicar's aunt cautiously peered down at me.

Relieved, I shouted, "Oh, Mrs. Wills, is the vicar at home?"

"No, he isn't." Her voice was distant and fearful as she tried to make out who I was.

My heart sank. "It's Lady Charlotte, and I'm in dire need of his help."

"Oh, m'lady, forgive me for not recognizing you. These old eyes are not what they used to be—especially in the dark . . ."

"Have you any idea when he will be home?"

"There's illness in the village, and he was sent for about

an hour or so ago. Someone was dying . . . now who did he say it was . . . ?"

I was frustrated—desperate. Where could I go now for help? The constabulary were at least three miles away, and I knew I did not have the strength to walk there.

"Oh, I know where he went, your ladyship, it was over to Dene Farm."

"How far is that?" I hoped it was nearby.

"On the road to Falmouth, I believe. . . . It usually takes him awhile when he visits there."

"Did he say how long he would be?"

"No—you never know with a death, do you, m'lady? The vicar usually tries to stay 'til the end. Consoles the family to have him present . . ."

Frustrated, I asked her, "Please, as soon as he comes in, please tell the vicar to go to the constabulary. Lord Penross's son, William, is lost, and I fear he may have been kidnapped." It was the first time I had even admitted to myself such an appalling possibility.

"Tell the vicar that Justin Penross has definitely been seen—also that I have witnessed smuggling going on at Tregoran Cove."

Mrs. Wills became so disturbed by the news I had confided to her that she shut the window with a bang, and I had to ring the bell again.

She opened the window a crack and called down, her voice thin with agitation, "Aye, I will tell him, m'lady, the minute he comes in . . . oh, but I fear it will not be soon. . . . Did you wish to wait in the vicarage for him?"

I longed to go inside, but knew I must return to Penross. Elizabeth could be in grave danger, and I did not want to leave her any longer than was necessary.

I told Mrs. Wills I would return to Penross and started to walk back toward the ominous graveyard. But the sight of it made me hesitate; I could not make myself venture through there again. I would take the longer way—up the long, winding driveway of the manor.

I left through the lych-gate of the church, and my footsteps echoed along the deserted cobblestone street. Overhead, the moon disappeared at intervals behind low, overhanging clouds, which foretold that the southwesterly winds could soon bring yet another storm.

The long, winding driveway to Penross, with its dense shrubbery and tall, sentrylike trees on either side, was almost as eerie as the graveyard. I heard the sound of leaves and twigs crackling—as if someone was walking behind the massive rhododendron bushes. When I stopped, the noises stopped, too. When I found the strength to run, the sounds gathered speed.

"It is your own footsteps," I told myself, grasping for reassurance.

I desperately wanted rest but was spurred on by the thought of Elizabeth alone in her room. A solitary raindrop fell on my forehead, and I looked up at the threatening skies. A storm was now imminent.

I kept praying for the sound of Lord Penross's coach coming up the driveway behind me. Perhaps, when I finally came in sight of the manor, I would see it parked outside the front door. But no such blessed sight greeted me.

When I reached the main steps, I looked up to see that my scarf was no longer tied to the lock! Panicked, I ran up the steps and tried the great latch. It did not give.

A cold dread now assailed me. How could I gain entry?

I ran to a side door that was used by the servants, but that was locked, too. So was the chapel door in the rear of the house.

The rain was now beginning to come down in torrents, and I needed to find shelter somewhere. I returned to the front door and leaned against it, but the wind drove the rain onto the porch.

I could not just stand there; I had to find some means of entrance. The only other way in I could think of was the secret opening in the eastern tower, the one I had found the day I had made the pretense of picking violets. Could I find the courage to venture there?

A flash of lightning impelled me toward the tower. I did not even know if the small door would be accessible, but I edged my way through the opening in the tower wall and tried the latch. It was open.

I breathed a sigh of relief and felt on the steps for the

tinderbox and candles that I had seen there before. Using the striker over and over again, I eventually managed to light one of the candles.

The stone steps, leading up and around the tower, were dusty and worn, and tattered cobwebs hung in profusion. My elongated, flickering shadow accompanied me on my terrifying journey.

I found myself in a circular room. Rain-streaked, diamond-paned windows looked out over the sunken gardens. The only furnishings were a chair and a large, round stone table, upon which were spread the remains of a meal. Chicken bones were strewn on a large pewter platter, and a half-full goblet of wine stood close by. It looked as if whoever had partaken of the meal had been disturbed by someone, or something, and had left in haste.

The candle sputtered from a slight breeze, and I cupped my hand around it—fearing it would go out. I turned around and noticed a door in the dark oak paneling was ajar. It led into a small, dark, windowless room that contained only a large oak chest. I stood in the doorway and held the candle up high, trying to determine if the room led anywhere. Then I saw another door in the rear of the small room. It, too, was slightly ajar.

Crossing the dark room, I gently pushed the door, and it swung open. A flash of lightning revealed the Green Room, the room where I had spent my first frightening night at Penross! I now saw that I had obtained access through the very door that had clicked open and terrified me so.

Walking as quietly as I could, I crossed the room, past the great four-poster bed, and hurried toward the door. There was a clap of thunder as I wrestled with the latch, but it did not give.

The door was locked.

In a fit of anguish, I leaned my forehead against the door. I knew of nowhere else to go.

Then, from out of the darkness, I heard footsteps behind me. Someone reached over my shoulder and snuffed out the candle. Petrified, I could not even move.

A mocking voice whispered in my ear, "Lady Charlotte, we meet at last! May I introduce myself? Justin Penross, at your service . . ."

22

Justin was standing so close to me that I could feel his breath against my neck. He swung me around, his hand in an iron grip on my arm. The room was in darkness, and I could not see his face, only sense those eyes that had so alarmed me before.

Then he relinquished his grip, and I heard him walk across the room. He lit a candelabrum and returned, the candlelight now illuminating his malevolent face. I saw a glint of mad exultation in his dark, wild eyes; the same evil sneer the artist had captured on canvas was now before me in real life. Justin had inherited the distinctively noble, handsome features of the Penross family, but they were marred by a contemptuous arrogance.

"I have watched you since the night you arrived, Lady Charlotte. It was not by chance were you given this room. I instructed Rogers to see that the Green Room be your resting place that first night. I had thought we could frighten you into leaving; I did not need an outsider coming in to make my plans more difficult. But I now know you are not so easily affrighted."

My whole being revolted at the idea that he had watched as I pushed a chest of drawers and piled my valises against the paneling in an effort to keep the door from opening.

Justin pointed to a chair, silently signaling me to be seated. Reluctantly, I walked past him and sat down. He paced across the room like a caged, intense animal. His clothes were elegant, yet quite worn; the cuffs of his dark green jacket were frayed. It was then that I noticed what he was holding.

"Ah, you recognize your scarf, Lady Charlotte. I came upon it when leaving the manor to follow you to the vicarage. Was it a futile signal for my brother?"

I did not answer him. Justin *had* followed me to the vicarage—and back again. He must have heard me ask for the vicar to bring the constabulary to Penross. Then why was he still here?

"I have enjoyed watching you all day, Lady Charlotte, in your attempt to find William."

"What have you done with him?" I asked in a low voice.

"And why do you think I have had anything to do with his disappearance?" he asked me, mockingly. "Mrs. Dawson and her son Tom are ill—or are they, Lady Charlotte? Could it be that they have taken him somewhere? Why is the blame always put at my feet?"

Justin walked around to the back of my chair, and bent over me, whispering, "But then, Lady Caroline's murder was blamed upon me, was it not? Why, in this very room they found her, lying not far from where you are seated. Strangled. In a fit of passion, my beloved brother killed her."

"Why would Lord Penross kill the wife he loved?" I asked, looking at him disparagingly.

"Because he knew, dear Lady Charlotte, that she loved me. Caroline had always loved me, but unfortunately she loved the idea of being mistress of Penross Manor even more. That is the reason she married my brother." He walked over to the window, and for an instant was illuminated by a bright flash of lightning. He stood with his back to me, as he had done the night I had mistaken him for Lord Penross.

Thunder now drowned out his first words to me. Then I heard him say, ". . . here, in the Green Room, each day. Such happy hours we spent together—and then he found us, and our secret world was no more. My brother fought with me and knocked me insensible. When I revived, I found myself alone with the body of Lady Caroline. She had been strangled. I was bending over her when the door burst open and the constabulary arrested me for her murder. And it was my brother who killed her!"

Angrily, he turned to me. "I have seen the way you look at him, Lady Charlotte. Love shines from your eyes. But be warned, my brother is not the person you think he is. I grew up with him. He was considered the epitome of what a lord of the manor should be. I always took the blame for any of his wrong deeds—and there were many. My parents thought their son and heir could do no wrong . . ."

I had had misgivings concerning Lord Penross—whether he had been responsible for Lady Penross's death or knew that his brother was in hiding here. But as I watched his brother Justin pace up and down the room, growing increasingly agitated, I knew that regardless of Lord Penross's involvement—I was in the presence of a madman who himself was clearly capable of murder.

"I hate the very sight of him!" Justin shouted.

He suddenly stopped his ranting and came over to me. "But all that will change tonight. Retribution for all the agony he has caused me will be meted out."

He sat down on a chair opposite me and leaned forward, his dark eyes flashing. "Do you not think that I have planned this, over and over again, for the past two years? Since I disappeared the very morning I was convicted for Lady Caroline's murder—into the swirling, liberating mists on Bodmin moor—I have delighted in planning my revenge. Oh, my escape from the dreaded Launceston assizes was quite a tour de force! It is useful to have servants faithful to your cause."

My throat was dry, my pulse racing, as I sat, terrified, and watched this man, who was mad with jealousy, twist my scarf in his two hands.

"Servants?" I managed to whisper, desperate to keep him talking.

"Ah, yes. You would like to know who they were. But that must come later." He stood to his feet. "Come, let me show you more of Penross's secret passages."

Roughly, he pulled me to my feet, and before I could fight him off, he tied my hands behind my back with the white scarf.

"Please do not bother to scream, Lady Charlotte. There is no one who will come to your rescue." He pushed me toward the door in the paneling. "This leads to one of the priests' holes for which Penross is famous. It has been most useful for me to be able to enter the house and live in the Green Room undetected. The bed, as you experienced, is most uncomfortable—however, I should not complain. Last night was my final, restless sojourn in it . . ."

The candelabrum he was carrying lit up the small, oppressive room. Justin flung open the large, iron-banded, dark-oak chest. "Observe, for this is where the wretched Catholic priest in hiding would keep his vestments and the accouterment necessary to hold the forbidden Mass—the golden crucifix and chalice, the candlesticks . . ." He looked around the small, dark room. "I wonder how many hours he had to spend within the confines of this miserable hole, while the soldiers of 'good' Queen Bess searched the manor for him. If they found him—he would indeed have need of a Mass!"

He laughed—a short, maniacal laugh.

"This would be a perfect place for someone to hide a person, would it not?"

I looked into his eyes, defying him. "I should think that, as the priests' holes are so famous, they might be the first place searched."

"Ah, well, then we must not leave you here, Lady Charlotte. But then, I did not intend to—I have a much better hiding place in mind."

He took my arm and directed me into the tower room where the stone table stood. Picking up a half-eaten piece of chicken, he thrust it near my face.

"Are you in need of refreshment?"

I turned my head away in disgust. He laughed and proceeded to devour it, then flung down the bone and finished the wine in the goblet.

"Come, we have not much time left."

He ungraciously guided me down the stairs from whence I had come, and at the bottom of them lifted a great iron ring in the floor. I saw a trap door with steps leading down into a murky darkness.

"You go first, Lady Charlotte. I will see that you do not fall." His fingers closed tightly around my arm.

With my hands bound behind me, I found it difficult to maneuver the steep steps, but he kept a firm hold on me until I reached the ground. Justin held the candelabrum above his head, and I could see a long, brick passage. The walls were crumbling, and water was seeping through them. There was a musty, damp smell.

"I am taking you through subterranean passages that are seldom traversed. This is where the water is brought into the manor from a spring on the moors." He laughed again. "Why, if I left you here, you would not go thirsty. But no, we have a distance to walk yet. I have other plans."

"Dear God, please help me . . ." My head was swimming with fatigue, and I was finding it difficult to walk. Surely by now Lord Penross must have arrived home, or the vicar had sent for the constabulary . . .

He led me on—it seemed for miles. The passages twisted and turned endlessly. At last, we arrived at a large, dusty stone room. Around the walls were cobwebbed niches, upon which resided ancient, crumbling coffins.

"We are beneath the chapel, Lady Charlotte. How beautiful you looked that day as you stood by the altar gazing down at Lady Caroline's flowers. Yes, I had placed them there, on the anniversary of her death. You were so close to me, I thought you might hear me breathing behind the gilded screen."

My face flushed with anger, remembering that suffocating sense of danger. At least I had not been imagining things . . .

Justin gave a grand flourish with his hand. "Behold, my late ancestors' resting place! Is it not sad to think of ending up in this God-forsaken crypt? Better to die at sea, if need be, Lady Charlotte, with the ever merciful tide lulling your remains with its never-ending song . . ."

Was that where he was taking me? To Tregoran Cove? How could I ever find help?

We were now walking down another dank brick passage. Rats scuttled across our path and into the darkness. I knew that I could not go on much longer.

He suddenly stopped me and gazed down at my face.

"You are beautiful, Lady Charlotte. You remind me of her. The color of your hair, the way you smile . . ." He touched my face, and I tried to evade him. Fiercely he brought me back to him. "Don't ever turn from me. Would you turn from my brother? I know how you have longed for his touch . . ."

He violently pushed me from him, and I fell against the crumbling wall. "I couldn't take Lady Caroline for my wife, but I shall have you . . ."

I shouted, "No!" and he raised his hand as if to strike me, but the sound of horses' hoofs overhead distracted him. We must be under the courtyard where the stables were situated.

He forced me to walk on, whispering in my ear, "Don't scream, or you will share the same fate as Lady Caroline."

A large storage room now came into view, and the smell of hay confirmed that we were beneath the stables. The candlelight revealed bundles of hay strewn on the stone floor—together with barrels, tea chests, and opened crates of silks.

"Guardian is safely housed above, Lady Charlotte. I borrowed him, in the event I should need to make a quick escape."

A trap door overhead was flung open, and I gazed up into the sinister face of Rogers, his steely polite demeanor dissolved into mocking laughter.

"Well, m'lady, I trust you had a pleasant journey!"

He jeeringly laughed again as he clambered down into the room, and I stared at him—not really surprised, but mortified to think that a servant who had served his master for so many years could betray him. Or was Lord Penross aware of all that had been transpiring? A thought flashed through my mind—Lord Penross was always away when the smuggling took place. Or perhaps he never really went away. . . . I found these thoughts distressing, and could not bring myself to mistrust him completely. At least it was clear that Justin's hatred was genuine!

Rogers whispered to Justin, "Everything is going according to schedule. The ship is now waiting near the cove. We have one more wagonload of 'merchandise,' as you can see, and Trigg will be bringing the money with him for the rest when he arrives with his lordship . . ."

Justin curtly interrupted, "We have not a moment to lose, Rogers. I have sent Harris to waylay the vicar before he reaches home and receives Lady Charlotte's urgent message for him to bring the constabulary here."

I understood now why he did not fear being caught.

"The rest of the contraband is yours, Rogers, to be divided as you think fit. Now hurry, for my brother should be arriving at any moment!"

As I listened to the conversation, I gradually discerned that Trigg, the coachman, had been making arrangements for the distribution of the stolen goods at the inns where he stopped with Lord Penross. And once, with me as a passenger, I thought . . .

"Did Ellie give you any money?" Justin asked quickly. Rogers nodded and handed him a large leather pouch.

"Ellie?" I could not believe what I was hearing.

Justin looked over at me. "Oh, yes, your faithful maid, Ellie." He threw back his head and laughed. "Why she and her parents have assisted us—even gave me luncheon in Falmouth the day of the celebration of the victory at Waterloo."

Now Justin Penross took my chin in his hand. "How exquisite you looked sitting in the open carriage in Falmouth, the pale blue bonnet matching your bewitching parasol." He laughed again. "Why, you thought Ellie's mother was ill—how compassionate and trusting you are, Lady Charlotte. Her mother is as fit as a fiddle, and she and Ellie's father have also helped us dispose of our—shall we say—ill-gotten gains. Why, without all their help, I would not be sailing for America tonight. A passage there is quite costly, but I have accrued a sizable fortune from all my enterprising endeavors. I shall begin a new life in the former Colonies."

I was shattered by the news of Ellie. Among all the servants, I had believed only she really respected and genuinely liked me, and I had trusted her. Now I realized how truly alone I had been in that big house.

Justin pushed me up against the wall once more and signaled Rogers to carry on supervising the loading of the last wagon. Men went up and down the ladder, heaving down kegs of brandy, tea chests, crates, and trunks.

Then Justin Penross clapped his hand over my mouth and said quietly, "I have booked a passage for you, too,

Lady Charlotte. We sail from Tregoran Cove for America in less than an hour."

Horrified, I struggled to get away from him, but he twisted my arm and roughly brought me back. "There are one or two other important matters I have to attend to before we leave. Forgive me if I render you silent until then." With that he stuffed a handkerchief in my mouth and tied another over it; in vain I worked my tongue against the wadded cloth. He then harshly bound my ankles with rope and checked to see that the scarf around my wrists was taut. Then, picking me up, he carried me over his shoulder to the far corner of the storage room and unceremoniously left me there.

"It would be most unkind if I did not give you the opportunity of being able to say goodbye to someone you hold dear."

Justin went to the foot of the ladder and softly called up to Rogers. "Bring the boy down here again—before the wagon leaves."

William appeared at the trap door—his pale, tear-streaked little face peering down into the darkness. He was bound and gagged also. My heart lurched at the sight of him, and I tried to break loose my bonds. To see the boy treated in such an abusive manner completely dispelled any lingering doubts I had concerning Lord Penross. If Justin could do such a thing to a child, he also could easily lie about a murder. I only wondered whether this madman believed his own story.

"They were just about to put him on the wagon with Elizabeth, Lady Charlotte, but I thought you would want to say a last farewell. Elizabeth was so unkind to you today, I doubt whether you would wish to say goodbye to her. Ah, yes, she and William have been sold to a 'gentleman' who will arrange for them to work for a farmer in Devon. It will be hard for them at first, but they will soon adjust to the rigors of farm life. Once they cross the Tamar River, Cornwall will be rid of the Penross family forever.

"I didn't have the heart to kill them—not children. After all, it is not their fault that they are heirs to Penross. But then, after tonight there will be no more Penross Manor to inherit. I intend to dispose both of it and my brother before we sail."

William was handed down the ladder like a crate of tea and flung down next to me.

"Your governess, Miss Marsden, has been so helpful, William, sending you to the stables this morning, and then persuading Elizabeth to open her door. That Miss Marsden—she fully expects to sail with me—poor woman." Justin turned to me and laughed. "I promised her a safe passage, but I unfortunately cannot stand the sight of her. It was hard work to persuade her I am in love with her . . ." He grimaced, then laughed once more, as he ran up the ladder to the stables.

My gag was so tight I could not speak to William, nor he to me. I signaled him with my eyes, trying to convey how much I loved him, and kept looking upwards, then closing my eyes, hoping he would know that I was praying.

He nodded and looked up, too.

Tears welled up in my eyes, and I managed to bend my head far enough so that I could touch his.

The men, one of whom I recognized as a miner I had seen in the hall at Penross the day the tin lode was discovered, continued to haul the rest of the contraband into the stables.

Out of fear, hardly believing God would answer, I prayed He would intervene before they took William and Elizabeth.

And I prayed for Lord Penross—the man I dearly loved and had loved even when doubts concerning him had sullied my thoughts. I was certain Justin had men laying in wait for his return to the manor.

Then I leaned against the damp brick wall, straining to listen for any sound that might tell me that, even at this late hour, help was on the way.

23

The last of the contraband was being hoisted up the ladder. I knew that as soon as it had all been loaded, they would come for William.

Stifled sounds came from behind his gag, and tears rolled down his face. I agonized—unable even to say a comforting word to him.

Justin appeared at the trap door and agilely swung himself down the ladder. Walking over to me, a broad grin on his dissolute face, he bent down and said, "You will soon be taking your last walk in Cornwall, Lady Charlotte. A secret tunnel leads from here to Tregoran Cove, and then our voyage to America will begin."

He touched my face, and I thought for a moment he was going to loosen the gag. "I cannot trust you, yet. Not until we are away from this place." His eyes plundered me, and I experienced a wave of terror and distaste. If the constabulary did not arrive soon, neither William nor Elizabeth—nor myself—would ever be heard from again.

A cry sounded in the stables, and immediately Justin ran to the foot of the ladder.

"What is it?" he called softly, his body tense and on the alert. From beneath his coat, he withdrew a large pistol.

"A carriage has been sighted coming up the driveway!"

William looked over at me, relief shining in his eyes, but in the next second his face changed.

"Come down for the boy, and take the wagon over the back driveway leading to the mines."

A swarthy man came down the ladder and grabbed William. The child let out a muffled cry, then was swept up the steps and gone from my sight. I struggled again to loose my bonds, but Justin's hands were upon me in a second.

"Lady Charlotte, we must now begin our journey to the ship . . ."

Untying my ankles, he stood me to my feet and walked me over to where two bales of hay were stacked against the wall. He kicked them out of the way, and proceeded to push aside stones that were blocking an opening.

"This will be a rough walk for you, even with those fancy riding boots of yours . . ."

Replacing his pistol beneath his coat, he grabbed a lighted lantern and escorted me through the opening into a tunnel hewn out of Cornwall's dark gray granite. Hastily, he turned and blocked the entrance with the loose stones, and we were in pitch darkness save for the wavering, sputtering candle in the lantern.

"This tunnel, which leads to Tregoran Cove and a disused mine shaft under the sea, has proved most helpful, Lady Charlotte, for we have been able to bring our goods up from the cove, hidden from the inquisitive eyes of the King's preventive men . . ."

In my mind flashed an image of the small boat anchored near the mouth of a cave in Tregoran Cove.

The floor of the passageway was rough and uneven and led sharply downward. Several times I almost fell, but Justin's firm grip upon my arm saved me.

The smell of the sea was becoming stronger and stronger, and I could hear the pounding of the surf. It would not be long before we would reach the cove. I felt numb; tears waiting to be shed hovered in my eyes but would not fall. In the last few hours my life had become a nightmare, and I prayed I would be freed from its ravaging hold.

A breeze coming into the tunnel from the sea blew out the candle in the lantern, and for the last few yards, we had to feel our way along the roughly hewn walls. We turned a corner, and there before me was the ominous Tregoran Cove, with the same small boat anchored by the sea.

The rain was coming down in torrents, and in the distance I could see a tall ship being battered by the wind and high seas.

Justin stood for a moment at the mouth of the cave and called back to me, "Our privateer ship awaits us, Lady Charlotte!"

The waves were so high we would surely be dashed against the rocks before ever being able to reach the ship. I looked around me in a helpless gesture, to see whether I could elude my captor and run from him. But he hastily bent down and tied my ankles once more and forced me to sit under a ledge, sheltered somewhat from the storm.

"We will be leaving soon," he said, then a distracted look came into his eyes. "But first, there is something I must do. An old score must be settled . . ."

I watched him run across the sands and commence the climb up the pathway that led to the top of the cliff.

My heart wrenched. I knew he had gone to find Lord Penross, and my heart was full of dread. Justin's hatred was so deeply embedded within him that the murder of his brother would seem like a warranted, justifiable act. I had to get free from these bonds . . .

I found a sharp rock within reach of my feet and I tried to cut through the rope binding them. My feet slipped, and I gashed my leg, but I persisted, determined to get free. Finally, after several minutes I was rewarded by feeling the rope give. I quickly kicked off the ropes and, kneeling, proceeded to work on the white scarf tied around my wrists. Once my hands were free, I tugged at the handkerchief tied so tightly over the gag. The knot did not yield, and so I struggled to push the restraint down from my face. At last I was successful, and I sighed in relief as I pulled out the gag.

I peered out from under the ledge; Justin was already halfway up the cliff path. My mind raced. If I could reach the path and hide behind the gorse bushes that grew along the way, perhaps I could follow Justin and be able to reach Lord Penross and warn him of Justin's intentions.

Suddenly, out at sea, I saw a flash of light, and then the sound of cannon fire ripped through the cove. Incredulously, I realized that the tall ship that was to convey

Justin and myself to America was being bombarded by what must be His Majesty's navy. I looked above me. Justin was rooted to the path, a look of horror on his face as he surveyed the battle—his well-laid plans were being destroyed before his eyes. Finally, there was an enormous explosion, and the privateer burst into flames, which lit up the sky for miles.

I heard a cry from Justin, and his face, now reflected in the light of the consuming fire, was twisted with mad rage. Incensed, he watched the fire consume his escape route to a new life. Then he reached for his pistol and continued his climb up the cliff—the wind and rain beating against him as if vainly trying to restrain him from his vengeful journey.

Not far behind him now I darted behind a bush each time he turned a corner. Then, looking up, I gasped. Near the edge of the cliff, Lord Penross stood watching the tall ship disappear into the rough seas—unaware that his murderous brother was only a few yards below him.

I cried out at the top of my voice, "Justin!" hoping he would turn around to me and not see his brother standing there. But Justin had seen Lord Penross and took his time aiming the pistol at him.

He yelled, "James! At last, I shall be avenged . . ."

Lord Penross turned in his direction. But before Justin fired the pistol, a volley of shots rang out and he fell backwards, rolling down the path to within a few feet of where I stood.

Looking up, I saw the edge of the cliff ringed by the King's preventive men, their rifles still trained on Justin. An order was given for the men to lower their weapons, and I stood in the driving rain, watching Lord Penross as he ran down the path toward me.

I could not move nor believe that I was safe. Justin lay between us—a formidable barrier, blood running from wounds in his chest and neck.

His eyes opened, and he looked up at me, his face now that of a frightened child instead of a maniac. "Pray for me, Lady Charlotte," he murmured. "I need forgiveness . . . I did . . . I did . . . kill . . . her . . . Lady Caroline . . . I loved . . ."

I bent down to him, and he reached for my hand, unaware that his brother was standing nearby.

I whispered, "There is One who forgave a thief as he was dying . . ."

Justin clutched my hand. ". . . too late . . ."

"No, Justin—Our Lord's mercy is as endless as that unfathomable sea . . ."

He closed his eyes, and his lips moved—I could not tell whether in prayer or delirium. But then his face relaxed. I felt the grip on my hand loosen, and his arm fell to his side.

In the beating rain, I looked up at Lord Penross, and in his eyes I saw no anger—only intense pity for the brother who had torn his life apart. Then he reached down his arms to me, and in an instant he had swept me up and was carrying me to the top of the cliff.

His voice was tender as he whispered, "Lady Charlotte, how I thank God you were not harmed . . ."

I could not speak, but could only lay my head on his shoulder and let the relief of pent-up tears be my expression of thankfulness.

The sun streaming through my bedchamber windows awakened me next morning. I sat up in bed, trying to recall everything that had happened.

Sitting in a chair by the fireplace was the sleeping figure of Mrs. Johns. Why was she here, and not Ellie . . . ? It was then that I remembered the horrifying events of yesterday.

My movements awakened Mrs. Johns, and she quickly sat up. "Why m'lady, yer supposed to rest, do ye hear?"

"Mrs. Johns, what happened to me? The last thing I remember was Lord Penross carrying me up the cliff path."

"Lord, 'ave mercy—you fainted dead away, yer ladyship. Ye were that exhausted, Lord Penross feared ye were ill. Why 'e even sent for the doctor—and 'e said wot you needed was plenty of rest, to get over the 'orrible ordeal ye 'ad been through. It makes me shudder to think wot might 'ave 'appened to ye and the children."

At the mention of the children, I bolted from bed and ran to her. "Are they found? Did the constabulary stop the wagon before it reached the Tamar?" My heart was pounding, and I felt faint at the thought of where they might be.

"Don't ye be a worryin', Lady Charlotte—they're safely tucked in their beds. Sleepin' their 'eads off, I don't doubt—like ye should be . . . 'Twas mighty late when they finally got to sleep."

I wrapped my dressing gown around me and without another word ran out of my room and into the nursery. William's door was ajar, and I put my head around it to see his soft, blond curls on the pillow. He was fast asleep, as if nothing untoward had happened. I resisted the urge to go over and give him a kiss, lest I should awaken him.

Elizabeth, too, was fast asleep, her face a picture of serenity and contentment.

I sat down at the nursery table and, putting my head in my hands, poured out my thanks to the Lord that these two dear children were safe.

Then I opened my eyes and I looked over at Miss Marsden's room. The door was open, and I could see two valises standing by her bed. They must have been left there in readiness for her supposed voyage to America. Where was she now? Had she seen the privateer explode in flames? She very likely may have escaped, realizing that her part in the plot would be discovered.

Leaving the nursery, I encountered Mrs. Johns, who was bringing hot water for me.

"Oh, thank you. I know it is difficult for you leaving the children, Mrs. Johns. Is your sister taking care of them?"

"For now, m'lady, but it looks as if—well, with yer permission, I'll be bringing them 'ere to live."

"Why, that is wonderful. But why do you need my permission?"

"Well, Lord Penross wanted me to ask ye if you would like me to be yer personal maid . . . seeing as 'ow Ellie . . ."

"I would be delighted—and most grateful, Mrs. Johns."

"M'lady, 'tis I who am grateful to ye, for all ye have done for me." I shook my head, but she continued, "Yer comin' to the prison, and seein' me children were all right, well, mercy me, I'll be forever in yer debt."

She gave a big sniff and averted her eyes. "I'll be going down now to see if I can 'elp Mrs. Dawson with breakfast."

Mrs. Johns moved toward the door, but I stopped her.

"Mrs. Dawson and Tom—they are all right?"

"Oh, a little bruised, but right as rain. Rogers and the Honorable Justin had tied 'em up and put them in the pantry—along with the cook and the nurserymaids and the chambermaids. Tom was able to untie 'isself, but couldn't get the door to budge." Mrs. Johns laughed to herself. "At least they didn't starve. I think 'e said they 'ad eaten nine roast chickens between 'em, and a side of pork wot the cook 'ad roasted and put to cool in the pantry, right before they were all tied up . . . As well as an 'ole round of cheese!"

I could not help but laugh with her—content to know that they were all safe. There were still so many questions unanswered—Justin had evidently told more than one lie—but for now the relief of knowing the children and Lord Penross were unharmed, also, was all I needed to know.

The thought of Lord Penross made me dress hastily. I looked in the mirror before I left the room. The ravages of yesterday were still in my eyes, but the bright blue muslin dress I had chosen to wear brought out their color and brightened my appearance.

I was about to leave when I remembered Lord Penross's book of Blake's verse. I turned back to pick it up and with it in my hands, I ran down the staircase, anxious to see Lord Penross. Yet, when I reached the breakfast room door, I hesitated—my heart was pounding so. . . . I took a deep breath and tried to regain my composure before opening the door.

He was sitting just as I had seen him that first morning, reading the newspaper, legs spread out before him, so deep in thought he did not look up when I entered.

"Well, Mrs. Dawson, have you managed to recover from your ordeal?"

"Almost, yer lordship," I answered, trying to mimic her voice.

Lord Penross looked up hastily—then jumped to his feet.

"Lady Charlotte!"

We stood looking at each other, unable to say another word. The depth of my feelings toward him were matched by the look of tenderness in his eyes.

He put out his arms, and without hesitation I ran to him, rejoicing in the warmth of his arms encircling me.

"My dear Charlotte . . ." he whispered.

Then the book of poems I had been holding fell to the floor as we found ourselves locked in an impassioned embrace.

24

*F*or the moment, yesterday's horrifying events were forgotten, and it seemed as if time stood still in the consuming warmth of our love for each other. The rapid beating of my heart made me feel it was impossible to contain such happiness.

Lord Penross finally released his tight hold of me and held me at arm's length. His eyes swept lovingly over my face. "Oh, Charlotte, I have loved you since the day you first walked through the door. . . . But I never thought you would contemplate reciprocating those feelings . . ."

"James, I did try so hard not to love you. But each time I was with you, my feelings would grow . . . until I could pretend no longer. But it was almost too late . . ."

Lord Penross took me in his arms again. "And to think that because of Justin this love could have been destroyed. I should have realized that your fears about him were well-founded . . . but the idea of his hiding in my house was so repugnant—"

I had put a finger to his lips. "Enough, now. We must try and forget, and not let thoughts of Justin destroy this happiness we have found. . . . Oh, my dear James."

A smile broke out upon his handsome face, and he leaned down and kissed me tenderly upon my forehead. The assurance of his love made my heart beat even faster than before. He bent down to retrieve the book of poems from the floor and then ushered me to my chair at the table by the window. Seating me, he placed the book nearby. "I trust Blake spoke eloquently for me, my dear Charlotte. I regretted having to leave Penross, when I knew how distressed you must be over Stephen."

I smiled, sadly, the thought of Stephen darkening but not diminishing my joy. "The words of the poem comforted my heart, James—helping me to realize that my Maker was near, and that He, and you, shared my sorrow. I thank you most ardently."

Lord Penross stretched across the table, took my hand, and gently kissed it.

I gripped his hand, trying to find words to express to him the intensity of emotions that I had undergone since receiving the letter from the War Office. "I have had agonizing doubts concerning my faith—agonizing upon all on which I have based my beliefs. I experienced feelings that I did not even know existed within me—bitter, passionate feelings of betrayal by God."

Lord Penross whispered, "My dear Charlotte, only He knows the hidden doubts, the fears and longings with which each of us lives . . ."

I nodded. "In spite of these feelings of doubt, when Justin lay dying, I believed, beyond any question, that he could rely on the mercy of God. I go on hoping—and relying on His mercy regarding Stephen."

"I pray your wait for word about him will soon be over, Charlotte. Knowing how anxious you must be, I took the liberty of sending a request to my solicitor in London, asking that he, or someone on whom he could rely, sail to Belgium and make inquiries about Stephen."

"Oh, James!" This sudden piece of good news was like a burst of sunshine after the many dark days that had assailed me since I heard from the War Office. "How can I ever thank you? I have longed to be able to go to Belgium myself, and have prayed that there might be a way. But this is indeed an answer, and I greatly regret my lack of faith."

He looked at me, reassuringly. "I too, have been struggling with my faith—have, in fact, for several years now. But last night, after you and the children were safely asleep, I asked God to forgive all the bitterness I have

173

harbored since my marriage to Lady Caroline, and then since her death . . ."

I whispered, "Justin told me of their involvement. I had no idea how greatly you must have suffered . . ."

"Ah, yes . . . the words, *devoted wife* were etched on her memorial for the children's sake . . ." He paused, as if recalling the irony of it. "But my anger toward Justin and the unfaithfulness of my wife, my unjustified mistrust of the vicar and the Church—everything last night was given over to our Lord. I am now a man purged of all my past. As I listened to your final words of reassurance to Justin—who, it is hoped, availed himself of God's forgiveness—I knew that I, too, needed forgiving."

He looked down for a moment and touched the book of poetry. "I believe I have the answer to Blake's question, 'What can this Gospel of Jesus be?' It's freedom, dear Charlotte—freedom from the past and hope for the future, for eternity, because of our Lord's sacrifice."

He stopped talking, his eyes brightening with unshed tears, and looked toward the view of the sea—the waves crashing forever mercilessly against the unrelenting cliffs. "Do you like John Donne?" he asked, Then, quietly, he recited:

Batter my heart, three personed God; for you
As yet but knock, breathe, shine, and seek to mend. . . .
I like a usurped town, to another due,
Labor to admit you, but, oh, to no end.

In a quiet, yet strong voice, he said, "Like Donne, I asked God to 'batter my heart.' And . . . finally . . . I willingly admitted Him . . ."

I shall long remember the time Lord Penross and I spent in the breakfast room that morning. So much was resolved. Firstly, it was decided that Justin would be buried at sea, for it was there he had expected to begin a new life. All the past, and the hate it inspired, would be buried with him.

Then Lord Penross heartened me by announcing he would no longer have to travel a great deal. The income from the new tin lode put him in a position to hire more agents to oversee the estates. Also, I wholeheartedly agreed that Mrs. Johns should become part of the household.

As we were leaving the breakfast room, Lord Penross took me in his arms and held me close once more. Then, in a voice that vibrated with love for me, he whispered, "Beloved Charlotte, will you honor me by becoming my wife?"

I did not even hesitate before answering. "With utmost joy I gladly accept your proposal, my dear, dear James!"

We decided we would go to London and be married there in a quiet ceremony. The only members of my family attending would be my aunt, Lady Sanford, and possibly a distant cousin, Sir John Hewitt, who would give me away—in place of Stephen . . .

Hand in hand, we went to the nursery to tell our news to the children. I was a trifle hesitant regarding Elizabeth—knowing her old resentment of me, I wondered if she would find it possible to accept me as stepmother.

Lord Penross and I entered the nursery to find both children awake and eating their breakfast.

William immediately jumped off his chair and ran to us, his arms open wide. "Papa—Aunt Charlotte, I still can't believe we're free! Oh, how scared I was that I would never, ever see you both again . . ."

We embraced him, thanking the Lord for his safety—and that of Elizabeth, who still sat quietly at the table, her head bowed.

I walked over to her and said quietly, "Elizabeth, I am so thankful you are safe. How are you feeling?"

For a moment she did not answer, and then she began to cry softly. "Forgive me, please forgive me, Aunt Charlotte. I do really love you. Miss Marsden kept saying that you were the one responsible for William's disappearance. I'm sorry for what I did to the dress and bonnet you gave me."

"I understand, Elizabeth. A dress can easily be replaced, but I am so grateful that our relationship is restored."

"I know I disobeyed you and unlocked my door. But Miss Marsden insisted I open it, for she said that Penross was to be burned to the ground last night—and that I would be burned with it if I did not obey her . . ."

I put my arms around Elizabeth and whispered, "All is forgiven, and Miss Marsden is no longer here to upset you."

Lord Penross knelt beside her. "From now on, Aunt Charlotte has agreed to teach you all your lessons—that is until we can find another governess . . ."

"Oh, Papa, please don't find anyone else." William rushed to his father's side. "They might be like Miss Marsden!"

Lord Penross laughed. "I will see to it that I do not make the same mistake twice. But be assured, Miss Marsden will never return here. She was arrested with Rogers and Trigg last night, together with Ellie and her parents. However, I asked that Miss Marsden be released and allowed to go to her family in the North. She was badly used by your Uncle Justin, and I think she has suffered enough." Lord Penross looked over to her room. "Her luggage will be sent on to her."

William volunteered to carry the valises down to the front door, but Lord Penross laughingly declined his offer.

Then he continued, seriously, "I am appalled to think that, for the lure of money, such trusted servants would all help your uncle mastermind the smuggling. . . . Also the plot to kidnap you and Elizabeth—to say nothing of Aunt Charlotte being taken to America."

He stood to his feet and ruffled William's hair. "If it were not for our young groom, Harris, their plans would have been successful. He had pretended to go along with the smugglers, but when he was sent to waylay the vicar, he instead alerted the constabulary and the preventive men. Then he waited outside the main gates of Penross to warn me of all that was transpiring. Between us, we overpowered Trigg, and handed him over to the constabulary as soon as they arrived."

William clapped his hands at the thought, and his father added, "We owe a great debt to young Harris, and I intend to see he is well rewarded for his loyalty."

Lord Penross turned to look at me. "If the preventive men had not come when they did, dear Lady Charlotte, I dread to think what Justin would have done. William told us that he overheard Justin tell that he was going to burn Penross to the ground . . ."

I nodded, shuddering at the thought of how close we had come to such horror. Lord Penross had not even mentioned that Justin was about to kill him . . . but perhaps it was best that the children not hear that.

He continued. "When I stood on the cliffs watching the navy bombard the privateer, I thought that you must be already aboard, and that I had lost you forever . . ." Then he put his arm around my shoulders, and in a voice filled with emotion, whispered, "Children, I have asked Aunt Charlotte to be my wife . . ."

There was an immediate shout of joy from William, and after a moment's hesitation, Elizabeth joined him. They came running to us, telling of their excitement and happiness.

Lord Penross and I hugged them both to us, and he said, "From now on, children, I pray that we will all be happy together, and put the terrible past behind us. In time, God will heal all the memories of last night—and of the past lonely years."

We stood together for a few minutes, contentedly locked in a circle of warmth and love.

The nursery clock chimed the half-hour, and Elizabeth looked over at it. "Papa, we've all forgotten—it's Sunday. We shall be late for church!"

We all scattered to our various rooms and met in the hall fifteen minutes later, as the church bells pealed in the distance.

Seeing Harris waiting for us by the carriage, I stopped before entering it to thank him for his brave deeds of last night.

Embarrassed, he said, "M'lady, I thank ye—but I did no more than was my duty . . ."

Our open carriage swept down the driveway, with Harris at the reins. I looked at his back, as he sat so straight—urging the horses on—and silently thanked our Lord again for the faithfulness of this young man.

Upon arriving at St. Michael's, I was suddenly filled with a sense of uneasiness. It would be the first time I had encountered the vicar since refusing to see him when he called expressing concern regarding my brother.

Lord Penross, the children, and I walked down the aisle

to the Penross family pew and proceeded to take our places. I noticed out of the corner of my eye that William tweaked the nose of one of the odd men carved at the end of the mahogany pew. He looked up at me, to see if I had noticed— a mischievous twinkle in his eye. I quickly looked away.

After the processional had gone by, I reached for my prayer book, and it was then that I noticed the vicar look- ing at me. He smiled—an understanding smile, that seemed to convey his continuing solicitude. I hastily nod- ded to him, and abashedly proceeded to find my place in the prayer book.

Later, as we sang a hymn, my mind went rapidly back and forth, thinking of Stephen . . . and of Justin. They were so different. Yet Justin's life had been torn apart by jealousy, madness, and hatred, and Stephen—whether dead or alive—was the victim of another madman— Napoleon.

Before the vicar ascended the pulpit, I saw that he was handed a note by one of the acolytes. He stopped for a moment, and then I saw a broad smile appear on his face. He took the steps upward two at a time and positively bounded into the pulpit. The organist stopped playing, and there was a sudden hush that came over the congregation.

"Ladies and gentlemen, it is my great privilege to be able to announce to you that Paris has fallen and we and our allies are in complete control . . ."

A happy murmur went through the church as people laughed and wept. Lord Penross and the children turned to me, each of them excited but reticent, knowing I could not fully join in the celebration.

The vicar interrupted the air of jubilance. "Let us pray, and thank God for this great victory."

Despite my sadness over my brother, I thanked the Lord, for I knew this meant an end to all the slaughter.

Ending his prayer, the vicar glanced down at his Bible. "Our Lord exhorted us to do what perhaps is one of the most difficult commands to obey—that is, to love our enemies. While we rejoice at the victory, may we find it in our hearts to pray for those who now find themselves the conquered."

I felt a twinge of bitterness, for again I thought of Stephen. Could I find that kind of forgiving love within me?

I listened avidly to the vicar's next words. "Our great General, the Duke of Wellington, it is reported, rode to the battlefield of Waterloo last month, the evening of the day that the great conflict had been fought and won. In the moonlight, he surveyed the incomprehensible carnage, which stretched as far as the eye could see. An officer who had accompanied him later told that tears had run down the General's face, and that he had said gravely, 'A victory is the greatest tragedy in the world, except a defeat.'

"Enormous suffering has been experienced on both sides for the sake of our freedom from tyranny. Let us never forget the great sacrifices entailed."

Tears welled up in my eyes, and Lord Penross put his hand in mine. Placing my other hand over his, I prayed for solace.

The vicar continued, "Yet we who call ourselves Christians have a yardstick by which to compare the sacrifices we humans make for freedom." He turned and gestured at the altar. "This brass cross symbolizes the ultimate sacrifice of our Lord. For He willingly gave His life for us that we might have freedom from all our transgressions—and from the fear of death. It is the same Lord who comes to comfort us in our times of adversity . . ."

Once more, I remembered the words in the poem Lord Penross had underlined:

> Oh! he gives to us his joy
> That our grief he may destroy . . .

Then the vicar added, "We may at times wonder why God allows the trials that many of us have to face. There is no easy answer. Many have lost loved ones in these brutal wars. But as we meditate on the sacrifice our Lord Jesus Christ made for us—His own life—we are confronted by His overwhelming Love. . . . 'Greater love hath no man than this, that a man lay down his life for his friends.'"

I looked once more at the altar. The sun was streaming through the stained-glass windows, and reflected shafts of light shone from the cross into the dark granite church—and into the dark corners of my heart.

It was then that I knew my splinted, patched faith had

been fully healed. Our Savior's love penetrated through my bitterness, and the wall of disillusionment was destroyed. If Stephen had been killed, I would still believe that God cared. One day, in heaven, we would be reunited. In my heart I poured out a prayer, asking forgiveness for my doubts and bitterness.

The recessional was being played, and Lord Penross touched my arm. I looked up at him and smiled—anxious to share all that I had experienced.

As we walked up the aisle, William and Elizabeth took our hands. The vicar was waiting in the porch, speaking to members of the congregation as they left. I held back, letting Lord Penross and the children speak to him first. Lord Penross guided the children toward the carriage and turned back to smile at me—knowing I would wish to speak to Mr. Ashford privately.

"Vicar, I am indeed sorry that I did not see you the day you so kindly came to the manor to offer your condolences."

"Lady Charlotte, I fully understand. When grief comes into our lives, there is a time when we desire to be alone."

"I was so angry with God . . ."

The vicar smiled. "A very healthy sign—at least it revealed you still believed in Him."

Somewhat taken aback, I smiled, too. "But today, as I listened to you I knew that I could no longer be angry with a God who loves me so . . ."

The Reverend Mr. Simon Ashford shook my hand. "May He bless and keep you, Lady Charlotte." His eyes shone as he bade me farewell and turned back to the church.

For a brief moment I stood there, with the warmth of the noonday sunlight upon my face. I knew that the fullness of that "Presence," to which John Wesley had referred, was now with me—the internal evidence of God in the heart of the believer.

I quickly walked up the pathway leading to the lych-gate, beyond which the carriage waited. Elizabeth and William were already seated, and Lord Penross stood eagerly awaiting me by the open door.

25

The next few weeks were filled with preparation for our journey to London and the wedding. A joyous air of expectancy now pervaded Penross in place of oppressiveness and gloom. Trunks were packed and the manor prepared for our departure, and finally Lord Penross, the children, and I bade farewell to Cornwall for several weeks.

Napoleon was now safely in exile on the isle of St. Helena. The triumphant mood of England could be felt as we passed through the countryside and the bustling towns. After years of deprivation and fear, brought about by the Napoleonic Wars, we would now be able to live at peace with our neighbor, France . . .

The journey to London took almost seven days, but finally the coach and four drove briskly up Park Lane. The city was experiencing a perfect late-summer day—the kind that can make all the rest of the year's adverse weather seem almost tolerable. The sun shone, the sky was clear, and the balmy air was cooled by a slight breeze. Riders in Hyde Park exchanged greetings, and many of the open carriages conveyed elegantly dressed young women with their mothers, or chaperones, eagerly watching to see if the eligible young men of the city would notice them as they rode by. It was a scene to which I had been accustomed in the past. It was five o'clock—the fashionable hour . . .

With great anticipation, I sat forward in the coach,

leaning toward the window to obtain a better view. It had been six months since I had left London for Cornwall, and the old, familiar sight of the park brought back intense memories. In a few moments, the coachman would turn right off Park Lane into Mount Street, where my family home was located. But there would now only be the faithful servant Jenkins to greet me. A sense of sadness swept over me, and but for the fact that Lord Penross's coach was only an hour or so behind mine, I would have reconsidered my decision to return to London for our wedding.

Mrs. Johns sat opposite me—dozing. It had been decided that her sister would care for her children for the weeks that she would be required in the city. But the journey had been most trying for her, since she had never been out of Cornwall before.

Elizabeth, on the other hand, was reveling in the colorful sights and sounds that make up the fabric of London. I had found pleasure in her company on the long journey. It had been a time of getting to know each other away from the stresses we had experienced at Penross Manor. William was no doubt keeping Lord Penross engaged in nonstop conversation . . .

The coach stopped outside the house that I had left so regretfully in early spring. Gathering my handbag and gloves together, I kept my head averted—almost not wanting to see my old home. I knew it was run down, and decisions would have to be made for its disposal. When Harris came round to open the door of the coach, I turned to Elizabeth.

"Why don't you go first? It is many years since you set foot in London, Elizabeth."

She alighted, and I saw her look up at the red-brick house. "It's beautiful, Aunt Charlotte. It's just as I imagined it would be."

Surprised, I looked out to see a house that sparkled. The red brick had been cleaned, and the white front door had been freshly painted, its brass knocker polished. A second look showed that the shutters and window frames had all received a new coat of paint, too.

Amazed, I stepped from the carriage and was greeted by dear old Jenkins. I extended my hand to him and felt the frailty of his—he had aged considerably since I left. But his face beamed with delight, and I saw him quickly wipe away an errant tear.

"Welcome 'ome, yer ladyship. 'Tis good to see you looking so bonny."

"Thank you, Jenkins. It is good to be home."

I hastily introduced him to Elizabeth and Mrs. Johns, and ran up the front doorsteps into the hall. I looked around in bewilderment, for every wall glowed with fresh paint. An enormous bouquet of flowers in a large silver vase sat on the mahogany hall table.

"Jenkins, this is hardly the welcome I expected. I thought the house would be in disrepair. Now I understand what Lady Sanford meant when she wrote me that everything was different . . ."

"That it is, m'lady. We've been quite busy around 'ere."

"We?" I asked, rather confused by his statement.

He looked away, a trifle disconcerted. "Well, it's not really for me to say, yer ladyship. You see, I'm sworn to secrecy, as it were."

He chuckled as he walked out to the coach and proceeded to help Harris with the luggage. I crossed over to the drawing room and opened the large double doors. That room, too, had been refurbished. The dust sheets were gone, and several more vases of flowers graced the sofa tables. I could not believe what I was seeing—but at the back of my mind I had a suspicion of who might be responsible . . .

I put my arm around Elizabeth's shoulders and led her out of the room.

"I'm sure you would like to see where you will be sleeping, Elizabeth."

"Oh, yes, Aunt Charlotte. This is such a pretty house; I'm sure you found it difficult to leave, to come to Cornwall."

We ascended the staircase, and I looked around me, still somewhat in a daze. "Yes, it was hard to leave. I grew up here, and every room has memories for me." We arrived at the first landing. "That door over there was my parents' room—where I shall be sleeping—and next to it was my old room, which I think you will enjoy."

Elizabeth put her head around the door and gave an exclamation of delight. "Oh, it is lovely!" She ran over to the window. "Why I can hear the horses going up the street . . . what a lovely clopping sound they make!"

She caught sight of my old doll's house and began to inspect it. I left her there for a few moments and walked along the corridor to Stephen's room. The door was slightly open, and I went in.

Everything was the same as he had left it—except that the room had been freshened, like the others. I sat for a few moments on the end of my brother's bed and looked over at all the personal belongings he had treasured over the years. His first Coldstream Guards officer's hat and his regimental badges were on the desk by the window. I walked over and ran my hand over the now-faded hat.

"Where is Stephen, Lord?" I whispered.

There was a slight tap on the door, and I swung round to see Elizabeth standing there.

"Forgive me, Aunt Charlotte, I didn't mean to startle you. I wondered where you were."

I walked over to her. "I think it's time we had some refreshments. Let's go downstairs and see if Mrs. Johns and Jenkins can supply us with a little repast. Knowing him, he has probably gone to Gunther's nearby for some of my favorite pastries and confections."

With her hand in mine, we proceeded down the stairs. She chattered on about the house, about being in London—and could we go to the circus one day? I assured her that we would; perhaps a visit there tomorrow could be arranged if we were not all too tired from the journey. We laughed together, and I felt the warmth of new friendship as Elizabeth began to trust and love me . . .

The sound of a coach pulling up outside stopped me from crossing the hall to the drawing room. I looked over at the grandfather clock and saw it was almost six o'clock.

"That must be your father and William," I exclaimed.

We both hastened to the door and, not waiting for Jenkins, stood on the top step as the Penross coach drew up. Excitedly, we waited as the newly acquired coachman, Thompson, alighted and opened the coach door. William was the first one out and came bounding up the steps— hugging both of us. His little face was beaming with excitement.

"Aunt Charlotte—Elizabeth—isn't London exciting? So

many people, and horses, and houses, and tradesmen . . ."
He rattled on incessantly, trying to tell us all he had seen.

I looked up to see Lord Penross alight. Our eyes met
lovingly, and he ran up the steps to embrace me. I closed
my eyes and felt the warmth of his face against mine. Then
still holding my hand, he bent down to Elizabeth and
kissed her.

"Papa, it's such a pretty house. Come see . . ." She
pulled him through the doorway. "Aunt Charlotte has been
showing me her room—and she's letting me have it for the
whole time I stay here. . . . There's a wonderful old doll's
house . . ."

She went to the stairs, but Lord Penross called out,
"Elizabeth, why don't you show William, and I'll be up to
see it later. I have something I wish to discuss with Aunt
Charlotte, first."

The children ran up the staircase, and for a moment
Lord Penross and I stood gazing at each other. Those dark,
magnetic eyes searched mine as we stood together—each
stirred by the depth of our love.

"You are responsible for all this, aren't you?" I finally
whispered, making a wide gesture with both hands.

Lord Penross laughed. "And how did you deduce that?"

"There is no one else I could think of who could be so
generous. How do I say thank you? I cannot describe my
feelings when I first saw the house . . ."

"I know how much it means to you, dear Charlotte. And
if you consent, perhaps after we are married this can be
our town house." Excitedly I nodded my approval. He continued, "I sold mine years ago—not thinking I would ever
return to London. I have decided I need to get back into
society again. I have been a recluse in Cornwall too long—
shall we spend the season each year in London?"

"Oh, yes, my dear James!"

He hugged me to him and then kissed me long and hard
on my eager lips.

Later, he whispered, "How I wish I could begin my stay
here tonight. My club is a poor substitute . . ."

Lord Penross led me over to the sofa, and sat me down
next to him. Taking both my hands, he kissed them, and
once more I felt as if I could hardly contain my joy.

His eyes searched mine and he went to speak, but hesitated, as if not knowing how to express himself.

"Charlotte, I have heard from my solicitor, whom I sent to Belgium . . ."

I gasped—almost not wanting to know what he had learned. ". . . Stephen?" I asked, my voice trembling.

"Yes, there is news . . ." With a gentle smile, he cradled me in his arms. "He has been found. He is alive . . ."

I buried my head against his shoulder, a tremendous sigh escaping me. "Oh, how I thank our Lord," I whispered, tears of joy now running down my face. Then, apprehensively, I looked up at him. "Is he . . . is he hurt?"

"He was badly wounded, my dear. A farmer found him unconscious and nearly dead. His uniform had been stripped off by marauding peasants, and for days the farmer and his wife nursed him without knowing whether he was English or French. Then one morning he opened his eyes and asked for water, and a few hours later he was able to give them his name."

I jumped to my feet, not knowing how to contain my joy. "When will he be coming home?"

"Next week . . ." Lord Penross stood to his feet and walked over to me. "But I must warn you, he is going to need a great deal of nursing."

"But he will . . . eventually . . . be well?"

"Yes, the army doctors have confirmed that."

I breathed a sigh of relief. It would be hard to see my brother so severely wounded, but each day would see him gradually restored to health. I still felt stunned—unable to fully realize that Stephen was alive!

Lord Penross said, contemplatively, "I have been thinking about Penross Manor. We have so many rooms that are unused. I would like to approach the government to see whether the old north wing of the house could be converted into a convalescent hospital for those who have been wounded during the dreadful wars Napoleon has waged. . . . It would be in thanksgiving for Stephen having been found . . ."

"Why, that is a wonderful idea! He could recuperate there, and we would be nearby . . ."

"The only thing that makes me hesitate is that you have such unpleasant memories of the old house. It is possible you would not wish to return. I have considered that it may be more expedient to find another country estate and live there."

"Oh, no, please do not do that for my sake. The past can be forgotten. Penross is your birthright—and William's." I took Lord Penross's hands. "Besides, there will always be a special place in my heart for the land that gave me you . . . and where I found the joy of His presence."

And as I said the words, I knew I meant them in my heart. Penross Manor no longer held any dread for me. Gone was the fear . . . and in its place was the greatest of all gifts—love.

In fact, even as I looked out of the window into the noisy, familiar London street, I was startled by a twinge of home-sickness. For already I was missing the turbulent sea and the wild moors—with the capricious salt winds rushing through the twisted, beautiful trees . . .